WILKES LANDING

SEAN MONAGHAN

Also by Sean Monaghan

WILKES LANDING

Chapter One

Alicia Brooks tossed aside the terrible document and peered through the little aircraft's layered window. The panes were slightly yellowed and cloudy and tiny ice crystals built up inside the face of the outer sheet of glass, making delicate, pretty frosting patterns.

The engine's drone cut through even those layers, and the sweeping whirl of the propellor created a blur that was at once reassuring and discomforting. The refreshing relief of a fan on a summer's day. The spin of a lumber saw in a giant, dangerous mill.

Alicia smiled and shook her head at herself. Why did she let her imagination do that? Allow itself to get just a little dark.

All she was doing was heading across Alaska. People did that every day.

Case in point the sixteen other people in the cabin with

her, though the ten empty seats suggested that the little independent airline was running under capacity.

It was nice, though, to have an empty seat beside her.
Right now she didn't need to be crowded.

Mostly when she rode planes, Alicia had too many papers
to go through to actually be able to indulge in gawping
outside.

Today was different though. Today might just change
everything.

No. It *would* change everything. Where the 'might' came
into it was whether it would be for the better or for the
worse.

Her father's estate. A complicated shambolic mess if there
ever had been one. Like a wrecker's yard after a tornado. Like
a hoarder's attic following an earthquake.

Like her brother David's garage on a day after he'd actually
done some tidying up.

Again, that carried her to dark thoughts. Would David
actually be there? Would he come and do the hard work to try
to make sure that these corporate interests didn't try to steal
everything away? Or most everything? Make sure their
father's estate was tidy and finalized?

And why was she thinking that she needed David anyway?

She was thirty-six years old, able to juggle multiple
accounts with demanding clients, able to run most days and
able to fend off the attentions of at least three of her single
male neighbors in the little condominium complex, and yet
still not able to handle dealing with her brother.

Across the aisle from her sat a young couple, the woman

staring out the window, and the man, in the aisle seat, reading a book from a new Kindle. He had earbuds in, which made Alicia wish she'd brought hers in with her. To block out the engine noise. To have a little distracting music going.

She stared at the back of the seat in front. In the plastic slot, above the locked tray table, there was a battered airline magazine. *Alaska Adventure*, with a photograph of those fabulous cold mountains in Denali National Park and headlines for the articles. *Braving The Waves: Authentic Fishing Adventures, Polar Bear Connections North of the Arctic Circle, Sam Strother– Actress Supreme.*

Behind the magazine stood a white paper bag. *Use in case of nausea*, and the aircraft's safety card. She didn't even want to think about that. *Brace yourself with both hands on the seat in front of you. Your life jacket is stored beneath your seat. Lighting will guide you to the aircraft's exit.*

Better to just look at the scenery than to imagine the aircraft plunging into the wintery pines like a blazing meteor.

Alicia shuddered.

The cabin attendant came by. A woman who couldn't have been more than twenty. Sparkly eyes and thick dark hair tied back under her stylish uniform hat. She leaned in.

"You wanted the soy milk in your coffee, didn't you?" she said.

"I don't want to be any trouble," Alicia said.

"Oh, it's no trouble, usually. Just that we missed getting any soy milk loaded when we did the changeover in Juneau."

Alicia's last day and a half had been one of connections.

Kansas city to Seattle, Seattle to Vancouver, Vancouver to Juneau, and now Juneau to Candleton.

"It's fine," she said. Probably not a great idea to have yet another coffee anyway. As someone who preferred soy or almond milk, she knew to be flexible and tolerant and open-minded.

A little advantage of entering her thirties and saying goodbye to a little of that twenty-something angst. And she had to smile at herself. Now thirty-six, she was no longer 'entering' her thirties, but actually closer to 'exiting'.

"Juice would be fine," she said. "If you have that. Or just water."

The woman smiled and winked. "I bet you'd like juice with pulp?"

"Sounds delicious."

"Coming right up." The attendant stepped back and continued along the aisle, checking in with other passengers.

It was a two-hour flight, and just one of two a week into Candleton. The little airline made triangles through Fairbanks, Anchorage and a few other little towns like Candleton. Somehow they stayed afloat, even if they did mess up getting soy milk aboard their planes from time to time.

Below, the mountains continued to glisten. The glaciers were smaller, apparently, though still impressive. Great snakes of ice, bent and jagged at the curves, rippled and broken through the center. The low sun drove long shadows out from the irregularities of both ice and rock.

Wasteland. Cold and unforgiving. Alicia reached up and

closed off the little air vent in the bottom of the aircraft's nominal overhead rack.

She picked up pages she'd tossed onto the empty seat beside her. A sheaf of a dozen or so. Stapled efficiently in one corner, and with two folds so that they would fit neatly into a standard DLE envelope.

It was all very straight forward. 'Herewith' this and 'party of the first' that. 'The assignee shall ensure that the aforementioned requisite documentation receives the required signatures before November twelfth'. It had head-spinning stuff. Gobbledygook. So easy to hide away some little clause in there that the wary might not notice.

'Your firstborn child shall be given as sacrifice'.

The City of Candleton—a joke surely, since the place's population was somewhere around eight thousand—wanted to erect a condo on the site of her father's home. He'd barely gone and already they were moving in. As if they had the documents ready and mailed them the moment he was in the ground.

She dealt with these kinds of things all the time, but with it all being tangled with her father's death, she was just... just... unable to focus. The words blurred. The meanings were lost.

Her father was gone.

That should be enough to deal with, without all the money-hungry bureaucracy.

Alicia leaned her head back against the warm, if coarse, fabric of the chair back. She'd kicked off her shoes and she sat in her stocking feet. She squeezed her toes in, as if balling a fist. An old thing, from some movie, to help with nerves and airsickness and concentration. Worked better on thick carpet, but she would take the functional, workaday flooring of the old aircraft.

Alicia folded down the tray table and made some notes in the document's margins. *Who cleans out the garage? Did he own all the junk in there?*

She'd only seen photographs. A skidoo, a ride on mower and a snow blower. Bunches of boxes, chests and barrels. Tires, skis, snowshoes, maps tacked up to the walls.

Where her brother got it from.

Alicia had kind of gone the other way. Simplicity. Eschewing things, living simply. Too many yoga retreats and too few friends. She might have a calm and spacious life unencumbered by a surfeit of material possessions, but somewhere along the way she'd become frosty and distant and hard to get to know.

Yay for therapy for giving her all that, even if it had never given her to tools or capacity to *actually do anything about it.*

"Are you all right?" the cabin attendant said, arriving with a tall plastic glass of pulpy juice.

Alicia smiled, feeling the stiffness in her shoulders and a tension in her neck.

"I should have gone to the Azores," she said, taking the glass. "Or Fiji or even just Cabo. Gone and lain on the beach in the sun until got too hot and then gone to the pool and soaked until I could appear in a California Raisin commercial."

"Oh?"

"Wrinkles."

"Oh, I got it already. But it strikes me that you're going completely in the wrong direction for any of those places. We've got a whole lot of the outdoors up here, but I don't know that anyone is slinking from the beach to the pool anywhere."

Alicia smiled.

"The place I stay in Candleton," the attendant went on, "it's got a hot tub, and a full-sized pool. Well, I mean, it's like a really big lap pool. MacGregor's Lodge. Are you booked there?"

The great thing about a small airline was how the attendants and staff were extra-friendly. Not that Delta or Southwest staff weren't, but it tended to be a little more genuine

"That sounds nice," Alicia said. "But no. I'm staying at my father's place."

"Oh, family time! That should be wonderful."

Alicia smiled and nodded. Friendly and genuine as it might be, this was no place to be talking about cleaning up an estate for a man she barely knew and never especially much liked.

Part of Alicia would have liked to have just picked up a rental car at the Candleton airport, driven via the General Store for matches and some kind of accelerant and headed straight up to Bondurant Street and set fire to the damn place.

She could have just stood back and watched the blaze light up the desolate landscape.

The Candleton sheriff would have been along soon enough, but perhaps Alicia would have been beyond caring.

"It will be wonderful," Alicia said. "In a cathartic kind of way, I hope."

"Oh," the attendant said. "Catharsis. Sorry if I misunderstood." She glanced along the aisle, almost as if looking for another passenger needing something so she could flee.

"It's all right. My family were never especially close. I haven't been back in almost twenty years."

"You left when you were a child?"

"Sixteen."

"You're older than you look!" Flight attendants always ready with a smooth bit of flattery.

"Thank you. Surprising, since I feel as if I'm rapidly aging beyond my years."

"You look great." Another smile.

Flirting. How about that?

No. Alicia tamped herself down. The woman was likely just very good at her job. Making people feel valued. Perhaps genuinely interested and likable, but still quite cognizant that tomorrow she would be making another two or three flights, with more bored, annoying and, potentially, nice passengers. People who were aboard for a few hours, then were off to collect their luggage, meet their rides and who would be exiting her life for good the moment they stepped off the plane.

For most passengers, the attendants were little more than window dressing.

"Thank you," Alicia said. "I feel as if I look a mess. Hours of traveling. Dealing with ridiculous documents—" she shook the sheaf "—and trying to placate family and friends over this little disaster. Which I don't need to bore you with."

Now Alicia poked her head up above the seat and looked along the aisle.

The other passengers she could see were sipping from their drinks, or reading books, sleeping, nodding their heads to music. One woman was crying a little, dabbing at her eyes.

"You have plenty to do." Alicia reached out and touched the attendant's arm. "And if anyone looks great, it's you. After hours in the air and you've not a hair out of place and you have a constant smile."

Good grief, was she flirting back? Ridiculous. Alicia was pretty heterosexual, she knew that. One time in college—practically a cliché—she'd spent the night with another woman. Aside from that it had been an ever-revolving string of male twerps, twits and, as Marie her Australian friend would say, drongos.

Alicia drew her hand back.

"I do have plenty to do," the woman said, still with that radiant smile. A little neutral now, perhaps.

"Sorry," Alicia said, placing her hands between her knees. "Thanks for the juice."

"No trouble." Another wink. Friendly, not sexual or anything else. Just doing her job. "Just let me know if you'd like anything else."

"Thanks."

The attendant stepped away as Alicia took a sip of the juice. The attendant looked back. Leaned in.

"Grace," she said. "I'm Grace."

Alicia coughed a little on her juice. "Alicia."

"Charmed."

Then Grace was gone, off along the aisle, and speaking with the other passengers in the same friendly tones. It was very easy to imagine her arriving at her lodge in Candleton and shutting out the world. Slipping into the hot tub and tuning out.

Alicia took another sip. The juice was really good. As if it had been squeezed in California just this morning. She opened up the tray table on the neighboring seat and nestled the glass into the little circular hollow.

The drone of the plane continued, but there was a sudden little turbulent shudder. Alicia looked out the window again and saw the wingtip bouncing up and down.

It was normal. Even in a small plane. Flex in the wings.

Normal.

One good thing about her brother David was that he knew about planes. He'd explained plenty to her over the years. Reassuring.

The whines and clunks were just the servos and actuators doing their jobs to adjust the aircraft's trim. The loud thumps from under the floor were the sounds of the undercarriage locking into place.

"You don't hear those thumps," he'd said once, "then maybe you do have to worry a little. Maybe the wheel's aren't down properly and you're going in on the plane's belly with... sorry, I'm meant to be reassuring, right?"

"Exactly."

Alicia wasn't a nervous flyer, but knowing that aircraft

were robust and had numerous redundancies was helpful in feeling more comfortable.

She was more nervous about what she might be about to face when she finally made it up to Bondurant Street. When she made it to the local lawyers' office.

It was a tough thing to process. Something best pushed to the back of her mind.

With so many other things.

The aircraft shuddered again.

A chime sounded. By the vent above, the *Fasten Seatbelts* lamp flicked on and off. On and off. Then came on and stayed on.

Grace darted forward. Almost running along the aisle.

Another shudder. Something screeched.

Behind Alicia, someone yelped.

Grace had gone to the front of the cabin and was strapping herself into the rear-facing steward's seat.

With a full shoulder harness.

Alicia grabbed at her lap belt. It felt so inadequate.

But it was fastened.

She pulled it tighter.

She looked out the window.

Something black was streaming from the side of the engine.

Oily.

Behind the engine, the fluid was igniting. Glittering sparks shimmered. They blasted away behind immediately. Carried off by the aircraft's velocity.

Grace was speaking into an old style telephone handset. Her voice was coming through the cabin speakers.

Alicia didn't hear a word.

Or rather, she did hear them, just didn't comprehend the meaning.

Probably something about bracing. About preparing to evacuate. About how everything was really under control.

They were definitely closer to the ground now. Ice. Patches of trees.

A road. That was reassuring. Perhaps they could land on the road and a bus would arrive to carry the passengers and crew on to Candleton.

But the road was crosswise to their trajectory. Left behind like the sparkling oil.

Alicia clutched at the hand-rests.

The plane shook. Another person yelped.

The seatbelt sign shut off. Chimed. Came on again.

Steeling herself, Alicia looked out the window.

They seemed so very low now. Hundreds of feet, rather than thousands.

There were houses, then. Cars. Yards.

The engine sound changed. Something below the floor clunked.

The sounds of the undercarriage locking into place.

One can hope.

Would this leave David to clean up two estates? Their father's and her own.

Part of her wanted to live through that just to prevent the kind of mess that would create.

The houses vanished behind. Then, a flash of icy grassy ground.

Then tarmac. Black. A set of white stripes like a crosswalk.

The aircraft's angle adjusted. *Pitching up*.

More thumps. Shuddering.

They were on the tarmac. Racing along. Landing.

No, *landed*.

Slowing. Almost as if they were on schedule and about to taxi into the terminal building.

Alicia peered out. The engine and wing were black with oil. Or oil and soot.

The terminal building was there.

But it wasn't Candleton. She could just read the sign on the roof. *Wilkes Landing*.

She'd never even heard of it.

Chapter Two

Brent Naylor sat back in the little emergency
building, sweaty, tired and achy.

Relieved.

A cool wind blew through, icy from its passage across the
wooded hills. The hemlocks and cedars, so thick and strong,
bracing themselves for winter. Their heady smell swung in on
the wind too, mixing with the stink of avgas and retardant
foam.

Brent was still wearing his heavy flame resistant overalls,
so the wind was welcome.

He had a Powerade bottle from the little kitchen fridge,
and he'd just about downed the whole thing. Mountain Blast,
the most popular flavor in the whole of Alaska, he'd heard. A
glacial blue, and overly sweet, but a welcome relief after a
frantic hour.

Around him the building stood austere and simple. In

theory it was a regular firehouse, with their relatively new
Striker appliance, a bunkhouse section, offices, training room
and all the gear storage. The little kitchen where way too
many microwave meals got cooked.

It was a workaday place, almost a home away from home.
Too many of the trainees and kids hung out for too long after
their shifts. Kind of the way of Alaska, really. Hanging out
and talking nonsense.

Especially after serious business.

The appliance itself was parked out front, ready to hose
down and check and refuel. The Oshkosh Striker, was secondhand but in good shape. The airport had gotten it a year back,
less than ten years old. Actually from an airport in Wisconsin,
just down the road from the Oshkosh factory. That fire crew
had received a welcome injection of cash for an upgrade.

And likewise, a little extra cash had appeared for the
Wilkes Landing airport. Some of it had gone on minor reno-
vations of the terminal, and some on actual useful equipment.

Some of the mining companies might be turning the
counting into slag and tailings, but they were happy to cough
up grants. Especially if it offset taxes.

Brent wasn't complaining. With a few tweaks, the *Fifty*, as
they were calling it, had been ready for duties.

The Oshkosh Striker was a pale yellow-green, distin-
guishing it as an airport appliance, rather than the red of
regular fire trucks. And unlike regular fire trucks with their
flat front ends, the Oshkosh had a steeply sloping, pointed
nose, to afford better views above and below.

It was a beautiful machine. Kind of functional and ugly,

but it had such capacity and versatility that made Brent envious in a way. If he was a little more versatile, then maybe he would have made more of himself. Achieved some of those things that seven-year-old Brent had imagined.

Starring in a movie. Flying to the space station. Winning the Indy 500.

But even the more pragmatic, more adult dreams. Finishing his degree. Staying in touch with his sister. Finding someone to settle down with.

Brent smiled and sighed and rolled his shoulders. Getting maudlin over those missed dreams was not a track he should go down. After all, he was a fire fighter. Willing to go into a burning building to rescue the children. Who needed versatility if that kind of thing was in your skill base, huh?

And the women who were impressed by that, never much seemed like the *settle-down-with* kind.

Right about now, he needed to give himself a good talking to. It was his job. And he had to deal with the adrenalin of a possible disaster, and the tingle that it left when everything was all right.

When the aircraft steps had wheeled up to the aircraft and all the passengers hustled off into the little terminal, he hadn't been prepared at all for his feelings.

He'd watched them walking across the tarmac. The mix of fear and relief had been palpable. Like the shimmer in the air from a chopper's exhaust.

They'd streamed past him. Confused and startled. Set down in Wilkes Landing when they'd been expecting somewhere else.

Business people. Students. Locals. An older couple that he'd met at a fundraiser a couple of years before, which was startling.

A woman with jet black straight hair and severe brows who'd met his eyes with her own ice-blues and given him the slightest of smiles and the slightest of nods.

There was something in that look. A charge. Odd, really. He'd never experienced that with anyone before. A pity it was all done. He wouldn't have minded a bit getting to spend a moment or two getting to know her.

Brent shook his head. That wasn't like him at all.

Out on the tarmac, the technicians and airport staff had taken over. Back in the appliance, Calie, his offsider, had told him the plane had been flying from Juneau to Candleton.

"Lucky," she'd said as they'd driven back across the tarmac to the fire house. "They would have had to have crossed the Fendals *and* the Cropper Range. Peaks up around eight thousand feet."

"A disaster averted."

"Yeah, and now we've got a dozen people not where they need to be."

"Alive. That's the key there."

"Man, we'll have to rustle up another plane or a bus or something."

Engineers would have to come in to look the plane over before it could be flown out. Likely the pilots would fly it over empty to Fairbanks or Anchorage for a proper inspection.

"Not our business, though," Calie had said, as if Brent had answered. She was very good at carrying out a conversation single-handedly. "We just have to be ready to hose things down and keep people safe."

That was it, of course. Even if fire fighting involved a lot of practice and a lot of waiting around, you still had to be ready.

Who'd have thought that almost before the appliance's fresh coat of paint was dry that they'd have the Fifty out on the tarmac attending an emergency?

The sudden arrival of the big ATR had been a surprise, that was for sure.

Wilkes Landing was a small town, and the airport mostly serviced the local helicopter and light fixed-wing businesses. Remote and mountainous, there were no real regular scheduled flights in or out.

Technically, the ATR wasn't a big plane. Down in Sea-Tac or LAX the thing would be dwarfed by the Boeing and Airbus jets.

But here, way up the valley, deep in the heart of Southeast Fairbanks you never saw those things. Maybe flyovers. Sometimes he would spot contrails. Perhaps from flights from Miami to Seoul or Los Angeles to Mumbai. People from Kansas thought they lived in a flyover state

Brent sighed to himself. He'd spent plenty of time in the lower forty-eight and honestly didn't miss them a bit.

"Beer?" Calie said, coming through the big open garage door space. "I think beer, don't you? Down at Gregorian. Beer and pizza. It's been an awful long time since I've had pizza."

"It's been all of a week." Brent finished his Powerade.

Calie was in her early twenties. The farthest she'd ever

been from Wilkes Landing was something like six miles up into the hills. She liked to hike, but also liked familiarity.

She was cute and funny and raw. Her thick blonde hair and green eyes belied her mixed ancestry. She liked to say she was forty-nine percent Inuit and fifty-one percent *who the heck knows?*

She lived in a faux-log cabin up on Jim Bales Lane, near the northern end of town. A quiet back end of the community, which backed onto a nice sweep of hardy old growth willows and cedars. Dropmore Pond was a couple of minutes walk from her back door and Calie often invited Brent and others up for barbecues.

Wilkes Landing boasted a population of close to nine thousand. A tight community, really.

Out on the Bayliss highway entry to town, some bored local had painted a line through the *Population 9000* number on the *Welcome to Wilkes Landing* sign and painted in *9001*. When the town council had fixed it, it got crossed out again, and *9002* was added. After *9005* the council just gave up. It was near enough anyway.

"So pizza it is, huh?" Calie said.

"Sure thing." Brent stood. He felt okay, actually. He'd fought fires before. Attended car wrecks and domestic incidents. Usually things were way worse than today.

"Are you taking any of the passengers in?" Calie asked.

"Taking passengers in?" he said.

"Sure. You've got space. I'm putting up a couple. A mother and her daughter."

"Won't they just go to Feihler Motel? Or the school?" It

was getting late in the day, so it made sense that the passengers weren't moving on. At least someone had figured it was safe to retrieve their luggage from the aircraft.

"The school!" Calie said. "That's cold! People survive an airplane crash and you just want to shuffle them off to the school?"

"The aircraft didn't crash."

"Doesn't matter. They're survivors. It could have gone badly and he knew it. Can you not see that?"

"They had a startling experience, sure, but honestly their lives weren't in danger. The plane can fly on a single engine. Part of its design redundancy."

"Oh my gosh, you are so obtuse. How have I never seen this about you before?"

"You have. And you've mentioned it before," Brent said with a smile.

A couple of months back, down at the corner of route two Caravel Road a pickup had smacked into the passenger side of new SUV. The SUV had flipped and, without touching any part of its bodywork on the ground, had landed back on its tires.

Everyone had been shaken, but there were no broken bones. Just a few scrapes and scratches.

When they'd gone down, Brent had made the fool mistake of saying they'd barely needed to attend. Everyone could have taken care of things from the little freebie first aid kit in the SUV's glove compartment.

"I have mentioned it before," Calie said. "And heaven help me, I hope I don't have to mention it again. Ever."

"Well, not until next time there's a faux emergency."

"No! That's exactly the point. There are not faux emergencies if you're the one it happened to. If there's a..." Calie trailed off, as Brent grinned at her.

"I get it," he said. "I do know what you mean, but some days I can be a little too pragmatic. I get that too."

"You know what?" Calie said, starting back toward the door. "I'm going to talk to Neil about getting someone to come and bunk at your place. Maybe you'll learn a little compassion."

Neil was the airport manager, and it had fallen to him to manage overnighting the passengers and crew.

"Calie," Brent said to her back as she stalked off. "I have plenty of compassion." He had to raise his voice. "You think that I got into this line of work with no compassion? I could have gone into hedge funds, you know that?"

But she was gone.

Off to find someone to share his little place for the night. There was probably no way out of it, so he should leave now and tidy up some.

Chapter Three

Alicia was still shaking as she sat in a corner of the Spartan airport terminal building. The seat was hard on her backside and she had the slightest edge of a headache developing.

She'd called David and gotten his voicemail. She'd called the lawyer in Candleton and gotten the answering service.

The air was turned up to warm, and there were still a few people around. The staff had been incredibly friendly and welcoming and apologetic. As if it was their fault that the plane's engine had just about fallen off.

Alicia rolled her shoulders and put her hands up, arms crossed, to touch her collarbone. She dug her fingers in.

Hard.

The sensation was good. Relieving.

She took deep breaths. She was alive. Everyone who'd

been aboard the plane was alive. Shouldn't she feel elated? Excited? At least relieved?

It was a natural reaction. Fear. Surprise. That adrenalin rush that had left her shaking like this.

She held her hands out in front of her and watched her fingertips trembling. Surely it would pass soon.

The building had a high ceiling with an enormous decorative lamp set hanging from the center. Pieces of pine boards in a clever vertical arrangement, making a kind of aesthetically uneven cylinder. The walls were a matching timber, in vertical slats in uneven lengths, giving the top, near high windows, a sort of rampart-look.

No. Like a ridge-line with trees making things jagged. All done with a reason.

Around the central area there were scattered sets of hard plastic seats. Four to a set, on steel frames. Some were in rows and some were kind of haphazard.

People were still coming and going. She was the last of the passengers. The others had been shuffled off to various locations with various locals.

Small towns. That was something to be grateful for. That wonderful hospitality and endless good cheer.

That had been her father's attraction to the place. Backwoods Alaska.

He'd moved almost twenty years ago, leaving Alicia and David with their mother back in Oklahoma. Alicia felt neutral on his departure, now, but knew that if she dug deeper she would find layers of resentment and anger and disappointment.

Things she wasn't ready to face.

Perhaps that had been part of the plane going down here in Wilkes Landing. Perhaps it was the universe giving her a moment's reprieve. An extra day or so, close by but not right there in the thick of things.

She smiled to herself. It wasn't like her to look beyond the practical and day-to-day. Some overworked and underpaid engineer might have inadvertently under-tightened a bolt and oil had leaked and the engine hadn't like that.

There was a practical reason behind it.

There had to be.

Somewhere north of this quaint little town lay Candleton, a quaint little town itself. The place her father had escaped to all those years ago.

She had visited before. Once, right before college when she'd been almost nineteen, and again about five years ago.

He'd seemed older and more tired then, of course, but on reflection now, perhaps he'd already been sick.

The semi-official documents said that it had been fast and peaceful, but of course that could have just been the very end itself.

Perhaps he'd gotten sick, gone into remission and then when it came back it was with a vengeance.

Why wouldn't he have been in contact sooner? Why did she have to find out through telephone tag with a lawyer?

Another breath.

There was a corner of the terminal's public space with a couple of bright, humming vending machines. Sodas and snacks. Alicia was peckish, but not hungry. At least not that hungry.

Uncertain, really. Couldn't think about food. Couldn't think about anything much.

If she'd been quicker off the mark. she would have called and found herself a place to stay already. And thinking of that then sent her into a little spiral of odd thoughts.

What about the other passengers? And were there really so many accommodation options in Wilkes Landing?

There had been council staff around, helping organize things. They'd checked in with her, but as a relatively young, single woman, they'd taken care of others ahead of her, which was just fine. She was happy to defer to families and older people of course.

So she'd sat in a corner going through the documents and sending updates on her phone. At least there were phone towers so she had bars and data.

The place felt so very remote. There were a couple of helicopters out on the airport's apron, and a few light planes. Service vehicles. A few hangars and sheds. A wire fence, and beyond that, sparse houses and then forest.

Like Candleton, really. Smaller, though, she had that sense.

With a couple of quick texts, she'd led Melissa and Olivia know that already the plan was going a little sideways, but that she was all right.

Melissa had texted back almost right away

No plan survives first contact with Alaska.

. . .

Alicia had texted back emojis. A grin and a snowman.

No response from Olivia yet, but she would probably be at the gym after tough day managing depositions.

Olivia loved training with weights. She'd actually held a local record by lifting one hundred eighty pounds. She was remarkably strong.

What was the time now in Tulsa? There was a big clock above one of the terminal's service desks, with a row of smaller clocks showing times in the big centers. Los Angeles, Houston, Chicago, New York. Then Paris, Munich and Vladivostok.

That Russian city seemed an odd addition, but on reflection, it was kind of close, in a general sense. Russia lay just off the Alaskan coast, though Vladivostok was far to the south. Alicia closed her eyes and tried to picture a globe. Vladivostok might have even been closer than Miami. Maybe similar to New York.

She opened her eyes again. Getting distracted.

It was almost a quarter after four already in Wilkes Landing, so after seven PM in Tulsa. Three hours difference.

Alicia fired off another text to Olivia, and stood.

There should be someone around to speak to. Right now it was as if Alicia, the last of the passengers, had been abandoned. Perhaps someone was going to show up with blankets and a pillow and apologetically suggest a darkened corner of the terminal for the night. Perhaps they would even bring a toasted sourdough salmon sandwich.

She should go and find someone, really. There were still people in the terminal, behind the scenes. She couldn't see anyone, but the building had that odd background feel of people busy with activity.

Doubtless they had their hands full. Telephone calls and procedure manuals to locate.

As Alicia headed toward the information counter, the glass sliding doors that led out to the tarmac opened and one of the emergency crew strode in. A tall, striking woman, with thick blonde hair tied at the back of her head.

She was wearing heavy, grubby yellow overalls and hefty black boots. Her face lit up when she saw Alicia.

"Are you the last one?" the woman said. "Where is everyone else?"

"Gone," Alicia said, glancing at the door opposite, that led out toward the parking lot. "Long gone."

"And they left you here? You were on the plane that crashed, weren't you?"

Alicia smiled. "I was on it. I don't think it really crashed. It was a sudden landing, but it wasn't even very hard."

"And yet they've still seen fit to just wander off without taking care of you."

"It's all right," Alicia said. "I can look after myself."

She rolled her eyes at herself, and so the woman could see. Alicia could take care of herself in downtown Tulsa. She could even take care of herself in Juneau or Candleton. But deposited in the late afternoon in another small Alaskan town was a whole other matter.

"I can tell that," the woman said, coming right over. "And

yet, how about I do my best to show you that South Fairbanks hospitality is not actually dead just yet? I'm Calie."

"Alicia." She took Calie's hand and they shook. Calie's hand was big, and hard with calluses. Her grip was firm, like one of those male manager's on a power trip. But it was different with Calie. Firm, but friendly.

"Pleased to meet you," Calie said, holding on and still shaking. She smelled of sweat and oil. Of the outdoors and hard work.

Of Alaska.

"Likewise," Alicia said. "I think they've gone off to find me a place to stay." She glanced at the entry door again.

As she looked, the swishing sound of the tarmac doors made turn back.

The aircraft was still parked out on the apron there. Someone had set up cones around it, with tape. Beyond, the big yellow-green fire truck stood, as if ready for the aircraft to burst into flames at any moment.

The doors had opened to admit another fire fighter.

The man she'd made eye contact with. In that split second, they'd shared something, but more than likely just friendliness and relief on both their parts, that there wasn't a fiery conflagration with aircraft parts and luggage and worse scattered along hundreds of yard of tarmac.

He wasn't as tall as Calie, but he was taller than Alicia. Just.

Shoulders that were thick and square and almost ready to burst out of his equally grubby overalls.

He had short-cropped dark hair, and an impish grin. His

nose was thick, and just a little crooked to the left and as he smiled, his left incisor was just a little crooked to the right.

But his eyes, though. They were simply captivating. Dark brows and dark, thick lashes, and his eyes were the deep emerald green of old, deep ice.

Alicia was clearly still riding the shock of the sudden landing. Normally she wouldn't look at a man like him. Perhaps in passing, but not being *captivated*.

And she definitely did not go for fire fighters. That was just too cliché. Fire fighters, cowboys, soldiers.

It sounded a little too like those Girls' Nights that Olivia and some of her other friends sometimes went to. Oh to be that uninhibited.

He strode across the tiled floor, his smile widening as he approached. He held his hand out.

"Last survivor, huh?" he said.

"What's that?" Alicia said as he took her hand. There was a sudden definite tingle there. And his hand was rougher and more calloused than Calie's, and his grip was just as firm. But in a different way. A masculine way.

A good way.

She gripped back too. Just as firmly.

Calie was looking back and forth between them, and Alicia let go, dropping her hand to her side.

"Brent," he said.

"Alicia. Last survivor, apparently."

He smiled. "Touch and go, there."

"Oh, ignore him," Calie said, putting her hand on his chest

and pushing him back a little. "He's trying to make a joke, but his sense of humor got hosed down a long time ago."

"Oh, I got it," Alicia said. "Bleak, but I suppose it's nice in your line of work to have survivors."

"You all are my first emergency," Calie said. "So I'm feeling pretty good about it all. Except for how all our people have left you here to your own devices." Calie glanced back. "Did you eat, even? Let me get you something." She headed for the vending machines.

"I'm fine," Alicia said. "Just trying to figure out how I'm going to make it up to Candleton."

"Oh, Brent will take you in his truck." Calie didn't stop walking.

Brent smiled again. Nervous, but charming.

"I'm sure they'll arrange another flight," Alicia said.

"I'm sure they won't!" Calie was now trying to stuff a dollar bill into one of the machines.

"They will arrange another flight," Brent said. "Of course they will." His voice was deep and full. The kind of voice that could do the voiceovers for those dramatic action movies. *They will... arrange another flight. But it only throws the survivors deeper into peril as they battle to stay alive.*

Alicia blinked. That wasn't like her at all.

"Are you all right?" Brent said.

"If he's telling you they will arrange another flight," Calie called over, "ask him how he would know. Is he an airline schedule expert? No. He knows which way to point a hose and how to do CPR."

Calie's dollar bill had been rejected twice by the machine, and was now whirring its way back out a third time.

"I do know CPR," Brent said. "And how to handle the fire fighting equipment." He leaned in closer to Alicia. "Also, I know how to get a vending machine to accept beaten money."

"I hear you," Calie said. "I don't know what you said, but I know you said something."

"That's me, always talking."

"Can't shut you up."

Brent gave a shake of his head. Smiled. Alicia liked the way the smile made his eyes crinkle.

Get a grip, girl.

"Did you offer her your spare bed yet?" Calie called. She looked over, frowning a little. "Actually maybe that's not such a great idea."

"I have a spare room," Brent said. "And I'm guessing most other places will be filled by now anyway."

"I'll be fine," Alicia said, putting her hand on his elbow, surprising herself. "I guess there's something happening at the school? Emergency cots or whatever."

She dropped her hand, mortified. She'd just survived what could have been a disaster and here she was *flirting* with some guy. A nice-looking guy, and a fire fighter to boot, but still.

Now was not the time.

She needed to get up to Candleton.

She didn't even know how far away it was from Wilkes Landing.

"Don't worry about him," Calie said. "He's harmless." The

vending machine clunked and whined, and she reached down to retrieve a soda.

"Harmless, huh?" Alicia said to him with a smile.

"I save bugs, you know. Calie thinks that's weird."

"It's a little weird."

"He'll see a ground beetle," Calie called over. "See it crawling on the appliance and he'll put his finger out and let the beetle crawl on, then take it over to some sedge or something and set it free."

"Back in the wild," Brent said.

"A good Samaritan," Alicia said.

"Through and through." Calie popped the top of her soda and took a swig. Lemonade. Some generic brand.

"The school will work just fine," Brent said. "They'll have soup and rolls and hot chocolate."

"Good then." Taking a step back, Alicia looked at her phone. She swiped and called up the maps and tapped into get a distance calculator. The app couldn't even find Wilkes Landing.

No, there it was. She had to zoom in.

Almost a hundred miles off. Direct. The roads looked as if they would run to three hundred. Probably not even paved all the way.

Hiring a car would be ridiculous. Hiring a helicopter sounded nice, but would be outside her budget. Even with the estate considered.

"Alaska, huh?" Calie said, peering over. "We'll take care of you, but don't go to the school. Not when there's a room available."

"I don't want to put anyone out," Alicia said.

"Not putting anyone out. You're in Alaska now. This is not L.A. or New York, honey." Calie put her hand on Alicia's arm, then took another sip from the lemonade.

Brent didn't seem convinced, but did manage a smile.

"Settled, then," Calie said. "I'll bring around my Jeep and run you over to his place. Did you get your bags?"

"Just this," Alicia said, pointing to her small red hardshell wheelie bag.

"Carry on only?" Calie grinned. "Practical. I like that. You and me are going to be friends, I know it."

When the plane had been evacuated, they hadn't been allowed to bring anything with them, but afterwards, once they were confident there was no fire danger, airport staff had retrieved all the passengers' belonging.

Calie put her arm around Alicia's shoulders and hugged her in tight.

Brent gave Alicia an understanding smile.

Chapter Four

Brent's six-year-old crew cab pickup was more than he needed really. It wasn't so often that it was loaded with people. But it was nice to have a little extra space, and the four-wheel-drive when he wanted to get out of town for a bit.

He followed Calie out through the back of the staff lot and onto Polward Drive, which led back into town. Clouds were rolling in from the south, which could mean a decent dumping of rain overnight. Maybe even a little thunder.

He'd lived up here for close to a decade now, but he was still unused to the weather. Growing up between western Texas and New Mexico, he was kind of used to storms, but much more to the dry and the heat and long, baking summer days. Even winter down that way was warmer than the height of summer up here.

Calie's brake lights flicked on as she slowed for the intersection with Tamarack. A logging truck was downshifting from up in the heights, but still quite a ways off.

Calie's exuberance was good. Part of him wondered if it was brought on by the emergency, but she was pretty gregarious anyway. Full of energy and light.

Matchmaking.

Brent sighed and gave a shake of his head. Yep. Typical.

Poor Alicia, in Calie's Jeep's passenger seat, would be getting a full rundown on him. How he was likable, but could be tiresome. How he was a gentleman, but could forget to hold a door. How he knew how to fix your plumbing but forgot which day he was supposed to come and do it.

Calie was harmless, but she kind of couldn't stand that he was on his own, despite the fact that she loved her own singleness. Just about relished it really. She got all she needed from some vicarious osmosis. There were relationship dramas in town that definitely needed active monitoring and massaging.

Kneading, she called it. As if she was making bread.

This woman, Alecia, was attractive, no question. Thick black hair with a wave to it, almost heading toward curls. Mischievous eyes and a quick smile. Sexy, even.

They'd shared that look on the tarmac, and he'd kind of put it aside. She'd just survived a traumatic event. That would always put someone's mind in a different place. And she was leaving anyway, soon. She would stay the night, then be on her way to Candleton to complete her disrupted flight.

But then, in the terminal building, there was something more between them again. Unspoken.

And perhaps best left unspoken.

Any other time, he might have enjoyed spending an evening with her. A burger dinner down at Ray's Fine Dining. A glass of wine. Maybe make plans to do it again sometime soon.

But in these circumstances, anything with her would go nowhere anyway.

"Brent, Brent, Brent," he whispered.

Getting ahead of himself as he often did. Back in high school, he would somehow manage to goofily find himself on a date and picturing not just the next date, but the next year and forgetting that it was just picturing it and end up messing things up through some dumb comment or other. Precisely because he was trying hard to *not* mess things up.

What he should have done was just said that Calie and Alicia could stay at his place and he could go to Calie's. A simple swap.

That would take away any of the awkwardness he was feeling around taking in a woman for the night.

"Overthinking things," he whispered.

Calie pulled in out front of his place.

About three years back, he'd bought it. A little, simple two bedroom bungalow on Spruce Street, in amongst other simple two bedroom bungalows. Trampolines in the yards and pickups in the driveways. Snow-blades tucked away in the garages.

Brent went around Calie's jeep and up his own driveway. He parked in front of the garage. Shut off the Chevy's engine and sat at the wheel for a moment.

There would be reports to fill in about today's incident.

Happy reports in a way, since it had all been very straightforward ultimately, but it was still paperwork. Brent was not a fan of paperwork.

That would be his sister, Jay, south of Albuquerque. Amazing how they'd grown up together, kicking around the desert, and she'd become an accountant practically there at home, while he'd fled for the ice and the drama of SAR—Search And Rescue—and fire fighting and, essentially, anything but the indoors.

Hard to believe that his sibling spent her days in an air-conditioned cube in a modern city.

Someone rapped on the pickup's passenger window. Calie.

"What?" she said, grinning. "Pull yourself together and come let us into your house."

Brent smiled and nodded and climbed out.

Maybe he could just convince Calie to stay too. He had an old air mattress that was probably still serviceable. He could sleep on that. Easy.

A buffer. Always a good idea.

Taking his keys, he headed around.

"You got beers in the fridge?" Calie said. "I know you do."

Chapter Five

Alicia stood on the little veranda of the little cottage. The place felt tiny. The grass in the front yard was sad and patchy. Dead in places. The air smelled sweetly of woodsmoke and flowers.

They were a long way from the Wilkes Landing airport. Seven, eight miles? Something like that. Calie had kept up a constant narration in her car, pointing out places and telling Alicia the Ed Wilden's house needed a paint job and that Collette Grahl had drunkenly crashed her pickup into the river two weeks back. Calie had all the details on who was behind on their mortgage and who'd won a halfway decent prize in the lottery and who was sleeping with whom.

As Alicia stared off into the suburb that looked like anywhere else in small town Alaska, Calie and Brent came around the side of the house from his garage.

"Not exactly the Hyatt, huh?" Brent said. "Sorry."

"Never really been a *Hyatt* kind of person," Alicia said. "More of a cheap motel or the back seat of my car."

She cringed at the words exited her mouth. One thing to be a little flirtatious, but a whole other to throw out something like that with a crass double-meaning her mother would disapprove of.

But Calie stepped up onto the veranda and gave her a wink.

"You've got your bag, great."

"Yep." Alicia touched the wheelie bag's extended handle.

"Inside then." Calie wrestled a set of keys from Brent and unlocked and stepped inside.

Brent waved for Alicia to follow Calie.

"Thanks." Alicia lifted her bag over the stoop. Calie had kicked off her boots and Alicia could hear her somewhere else in the house already.

"Are you two dating?" Alicia said, stopping and lifting one foot to untie her shoelaces.

"Dating? Us? Nope. You don't need to take off your shoes." Already Brent was removing his. "Work boots," he said. "We've been out all over the tarmac and so on. You're fine."

"It feels polite," she said.

"Texas?"

"Oklahoma."

"There you go." His grin was warm and almost goofy. Friendly. She didn't have a thing to worry about.

Alicia finished untying and slipped off both of her trainers.

"Come on," Brent said. "Before Calie takes the last of everything out of my fridge."

"Hey!" Calie said, stepping into the hallway from, presumably, the kitchen. She was holding a slim green beer, and she held it out to Alicia.

"Heineken?" Calie said. "National beer of Alaska."

Alicia smiled and accepted the bottle. She had the sense that whichever beer Calie was holding would be considered the 'National beer of Alaska' in that moment. Budweiser, Stumps, whatever.

"Thanks," Alicia said. "But, isn't it the two of you who've earned this? Me I just flew in to the wrong town."

"Nah," Calie said, turning back to the kitchen. "You, my girl, are right where you need to be. Listen up Brent, you need a shower, and even though you have a guest, you still got to go first."

"I wouldn't want to hog it." Brent followed Calie through. "Guests first."

"No, no," Alicia said, following him into the kitchen. "Go ahead."

The kitchen was bright, if compact. A gas oven and stovetop, microwave, a nice stainless steel coffee maker that seemed a bit elaborate for a single man.

Perhaps he wasn't single. Perhaps he was recently divorced, with a couple of kids.

Alicia took a sip of the beer, cringing at herself again. His domestic situation was hardly any of her business. He'd offered a place for her to stay.

Tomorrow she would be on another plane on the way to Candleton.

The beer was cold and refreshing. Just right. Who'd have thought she needed it?

Well. Calie, clearly.

And Calie was right. Brent was sweaty and the smell was strong. Musky and alluring, but it would get overpowering soon.

"See?" Calie said to Brent.

"And you too, Calie," Alicia said. "You need to shower."

"Me! Girls don't sweat. We gl–"

"Enough," Alicia said. "How far away do you live?"

"What? Why?"

"Just figuring out if it's quicker to send you home to shower up, or if you should just shower here."

Calie brightened. "Hear that, Brent? She's already taking over with the whole shower roster. That's a keeper. You sure you need to go to Candleton, Alicia? We could use someone like you right here in town."

Alicia laughed. "Yeah. I really do have to get up there." She was feeling more relaxed now. The whole complement of passengers should have had Calie around. Her almost silly energy was quite uplifting.

And still, there was the sad business in Candleton that needed to get done. Quickly.

"You sure you have to get up there?" Calie said. "Really? Stick around."

"Calie, come on," Brent said.

"It's all right," Alicia said. "But I do have family business. Kind of needs to be finished. 'Yesterday', as they say."

"Really? What is–"

"Calie," Brent said. "Let the poor woman be. It's personal."

"Right, because it being personal stops me dead, huh?"

"It doesn't, always, but it should."

Alicia took a breath.

"My father died," she said. "I have to get up there to tidy his property and sort out the remnants of the estate."

"Oh," Calie said, suddenly mortified. "I'm so sorry for your... sorry that happened."

"Don't be. It's fine. We didn't have much contact over the last ten or so years."

"Sorry to hear that," Brent said.

Alicia shrugged. "He had his life, I had mine." That sounded bitter and callous. She closed her eyes a moment. Here she was with these two kind people who were taking care of her after a scare, but she was still wrapped up in this whole thing with her dad.

"Sorry," she whispered.

"Oh, nothin' to be sorry about hun'," Calie said. "You and me and half of just about everyone I know have every right to be mad at their dad. Other half, I don't know about, but hey. How about you Brent?"

"Calie."

"You get on all right with your father?"

"Sure."

"Lucky."

"Calie, go home. Take a shower. A long shower. Come on back and I'll stick a pizza in the oven or something. We can chill."

Calie looked at Alicia. "Alaska joke. Chill. Get it?"

"I get it."

"All right. I'd hug you, but I'm sweaty and grubby. I'll see you in a half hour, all scrubbed and wearing something ten thousand times more stylish than these overalls. Goodness knows, I should have just showered at the station-house. Oh, wait, the bathroom is busted and we haven't gotten someone in to fix it yet. Who was it that was arranging that, I wonder?"

"Calie," Brent said. "Get out. Keep that up and I'll disinvite you for pizza."

"Got it." Calie raised her hands. "And it's 'uninvite', not 'disinvite'."

Brent glared at her and Calie scampered back out to the hallway.

A moment later came the sound of the front door closing.

Alicia took another sip of the beer and gave Brent a smile. "You and me, huh?"

Brent smiled. She did like the way it made his eyes crinkle up.

"You and me," he said. "Make yourself at home. There are snacks and stuff in the middle cupboard above the sink, but I'll make pizza when I'm done in the shower." He made a show of turning his head to sniff at his armpit. "I might be a little while."

He flashed her that wonderful smile and went out through to the hallway.

Wonderful smile. She clearly had had a traumatic experience and was processing through that. Well, she could give herself the night, then she needed to be over it and back into the practicalities of the situation.

A hundreds miles away from where she needed to be and behind schedule.

From the bathroom along the hallway came the bustling, rustling sounds of Brent stripping off and running the shower. Good grief, was he doing that with the door open? Single men living on their own, forgetting that they had guests.

Alicia took another good sip from the beer and started to explore.

Sure enough, there were snacks in the middle cupboard. Doritos and Pringles and a huge bag of generic corn chips. Crackers and sweet cookies. A six pack of Coke cans.

More cans in the fridge, but mostly beer. Spreads and bread rolls and pasta. Some actual vegetables.

She closed the door. No sense in having him appear at the kitchen door to find her with her nose in his fridge.

The kitchen was separated from the living room by a set of double doors. Brent had a single, wide sofa facing a large television mounted low on the wall. His fireplace was large and cheery and welcoming. The kind of room where it would be lovely to snuggle back with hot chocolate and a blazing fire and a lightweight movie.

Across the hallway from the living room lay the spare room. A double bed, made up nicely, with a bookcase stocked with long rows of paperbacks. John Grisham and Norah Roberts and David Baldacci, among others. The guy was a reader, though she never would have pegged him as a Norah Roberts kind of guy.

Alicia smiled to herself again. This was just some guy who worked as a fire fighter in Wilkes Landing, Alaska. A guy who was nice enough to let her stay for the night. A guy she'd met all of an hour ago.

Hopeless.

But she'd known it. Well, known something. The moment their eyes had met when everyone was exiting the landed aircraft and there he was on the tarmac, helping to keep things safe.

Their eyes had met.

The briefest of catches in it. The sensible, pragmatic part of her knew not to read too much into it. After all, she made eye contact with people every day. Sometimes dozens of people.

It never met anything more than just regular human contact.

But this moment, some other part of her knew, meant something different. As if there was a deeper connection there waiting to be uncovered.

And then the universe had delivered him right to her. Or her to him.

Her friend Olivia would like that. She was always divining the reasons between why seemingly random things happened.

From the hallway came the sound of the shower shutting off.

Alicia stepped back from the spare room's doorway and slipped into the lounge. Still holding the beer, she sat in the sofa, facing the television. Innocent, rather than inquisitive. Waiting, rather than exploring.

As if he might believe that.

The creak of a door, then the sound of footfalls. He looked in through the door to the kitchen dining room.

Wearing just a towel around his waist. His hair was wet and tousled. Both on his head and muscled chest. Dark, curly hair. Just thick enough.

Alicia had to concentrate so she didn't spill her beer.

"Here you are," he said. "Sorry, I should have said, but the spare room's in front. You can toss your stuff in there and set up. I imagine you want to go to bed right way." He closed his eyes. "To sleep. Go to sleep right away."

She smiled at his discomfort.

"Bed soon sounds good," she said. Flirtatious. What had gotten into her?

"I can rustle up a snack," he said, clearly trying to ignore his faux pas, and her response. "Rather than making pizza."

"Pizza sounds good. And if I go to bed, I won't sleep. Too keyed up. Later is better. Food and beer, then sleep." She almost added 'alone', but held her tongue. *That* should be obvious.

"Thanks," she added.

"Yep. I'll put out a towel and washcloth for you. Soap's there, and shampoo, though I guess you might have your own. Watch the shower mixer tap, it tends to do a little jump from just about warm enough to too hot. Aim for seven o'clock."

"Seven o'clock. Got it." The lounge room had a low wooden coffee table with coasters that had photographs of Alaska. She set her beer down on a grizzly bear scooping a salmon from a river, and stood. There was tension in her shoulders. A shower would be great, and too hot might be just about right.

Brent was still standing in the doorway. Just looking at her. She smiled at him.

"You might, sir," she said, "want to go put on some clothes."

He looked down as if suddenly realizing that he had on just a towel.

"I might, yes," he said.

Chapter Six

In his bedroom, Brent toweled dry.

Idiot.

Standing there staring at her like a slavering teenager, *while only wearing a towel*.

He was conscious of his chest hair. He'd gotten hairy when he actually had only just been a teen. Fourteen, and his chest had quickly thickened with dark curls as if he had a little gorilla DNA tucked away in a corner somewhere.

He looked at himself in the closet door mirror.

He wasn't good-looking enough to ever pose for one of those Fire-Fighters of Alaska calendars, but he had the right kind of physique. Almost. Shoulders a little too broad, hips a little too narrow, fingers just a little too long. But he stood just a shade over six foot. Tall but not too tall.

Sweetheart Calie was taller and she really knew how to carry her height. She would stride into the blazes on their training days, telling everyone that things were under control. Her size became reassuring. Larger than life, as they say.

Brent dressed quickly. Levi's 501s, a pair of simple Converse high top sneakers and a plain white tee shirt.

He checked the mirror and the shirt was just a little too tight, which would make it look as if he was trying to show off his pecs and shoulders. He switched it out for a Coldplay tour shirt from a few years back.

He and Mason from MacArthur's Lumber and a couple of other guys had flown down to Seattle for a long weekend. The concert had been amazing, and they'd taken the chance to take a fishing charter out on the harbor and to play eighteen holes down at Tacoma.

Mason had been killed soon after in a forestry accident. In a way it was bittersweet wearing the shirt. It had been his idea that they all cough up the extra dollars for the matching souvenirs.

"When are you ever going to get to see them again?" Mason had said at the time.

His loss still stung, that was for sure.

The Coldplay shirt looked a thousand times better than his first choice. Black fabric, but with bold, playful colors in the print design.

The shower was still running when he returned to the kitchen. Good. She was making herself at home. He almost went to take a look in the guest bedroom, but he resisted. It was her space for the duration now. None of his business.

He set to making a pizza. He had frozen bases, of course—he was a bachelor—and little pots of tomato paste and a bag of grated cheese. A pack of sliced salami which had been in the fridge a while, but that stuff never went off. He gave it a sniff anyway. Fine.

Vegetables were another issue. He had an onion, and a jar of olives, and he found a can of pineapple rings in back of a cupboard.

Maybe she had Italian heritage, given those piercing eyes and thick dark hair, and maybe she would be offended by pineapple on a pizza.

Working quickly, he assembled things on the base, leaving off the pineapple. The oven was already up to heat and he slid the tray with the pizza in. Set the timer.

The bathroom door opened and Alicia padded by along the hallway. She had her hair up in a towel and another towel around her chest and waist. She didn't even look into the kitchen.

"Pizza's just gone in," he called. "I guess it'll take—"

The sound of the front door opening cut him off. Then Calie's voice. Exuberant again.

Maybe the emergency actually amped her up.

Brent listened to Calie and Alicia talking, without being able to make out any of the words. Perhaps for the best. It was easy to imagine Calie working on the poor woman to stay a little longer.

Bending, he peered into the oven to see how the pizza was doing. It still looked the same. After a minute or so, what a surprise.

He found the beer he'd opened earlier and left on the bench and took another swig. He'd gotten better with beer, that was for sure. Mostly just sipping and on the rare occasions where he opened a second, he never finished it.

The last time he'd let loose had been that concert in Seattle. Never again, that was for sure. He was too old, both metabolically—hangovers in your thirties were atrocious—and in terms of maintaining his dignity. Twenty-somethings could get away with making jerks of themselves, but older than that and it was just plain unbecoming.

"Well," Calie said, coming through. "Did you set fire to the pizza yet?"

"Not me," he said, looking around. "I put fires out, remember?"

It was an old joke, but they never tired of it

Calie was wearing a floral dress that suited her figure. Square shoulders and flared nicely from the hips. The hem was below her knees and on her feet she wore a pair of heavy black Dr. Martins boots. The perfect ensemble. The flowers were so vivid and strong that Brent could practically smell the floral scent.

"You were quick," he said.

"Had to be. Someone needs to protect poor Alicia from your misguided masculine 'charms'." How was Calie able to actually pronounce a word so that it sounded as if it was in quote marks? Most people had to do air quotes with their fingers.

"Maybe someone needs to protect me from your meddling tendencies."

"Ouch! You wound me!" Calie clutched at her sternum.

"So dramatic. Did you have time for shopping somehow?"

Calie was carrying a plastic shopping bag from Page's, the little local general store.

"Nope," she said. "But I had some salad in the fridge and I figure that counteracts some of the effects of pizza. Especially the kind of pizza you would make."

"What does that mean?"

"Too much cheese, too much sauce, too much salami."

Well she had that right.

"What's so dramatic?" Alicia said, appearing at the kitchen door. She was wearing jeans and a Coldplay tour shirt.

Calie looked back and forth between them.

"Oh," Alicia said, noticing Brent's shirt.

"Yeah," Brent said.

"That's all the two of you can say? Really? Is this not like a kind of perfect serendipity?"

"Different tours," Alicia said. "Brent's is from a couple of years back, but mine's from a few years earlier."

"Exactly right," Brent said.

"Omigosh!" Calie's eyes were wide enough to drive the fire appliance straight through. "That the two of you would even know that is both disturbing and so sweet!"

"They're just a band," Alicia said. "They came through OKC so we went."

"So *sweet*." Calie clasped her hands at her chin.

"Pizza smells good," Alicia said.

"House special." Brent turned to the oven and checked through the glass. The cheese was just starting to look shiny as it began to melt, but it wasn't bubbling yet.

More importantly it gave him a moment to avoid looking into Alicia's fabulous playful eyes.

Which he would have loved to have done, but with Calie right there, a sudden wave of nerves washed over him.

Calie was right, though. It was cute that they essentially had matching shirts. It was a nice point of continuity that would make for a great conversation starter. *What's your favorite song? How was the light show? Did they play enough old stuff?*

Not continuity. Synchronicity. Or commonality. That was it.

He smiled to himself. Was he getting flustered?

"Ah, Brent," Calie said. "The pizza's not going to cook any faster if you watch it."

Brent stood. Both women were watching him with amused expressions.

Great.

"What's the salad, then?" he said.

Which right away took the focus off him.

Then the kitchen became bustling as both Calie and Alicia began preparing the table with plates and utensils. Calie raided the fridge for more beers and sauces.

Soon they were all sitting around the table with slices of too-cheesy pizza with a base that was a little too crisp.

Calie told stories about her times growing up in Anchorage and Juneau and out in the wilds of British Colombia. About the old F150 she'd bought with a wound-back clock, a spongey chassis and enough fiberglass in its panels to build a boat.

"Got rid of that thing real fast," she said.

The pizza cheese was stringy and tasty and the sauce was just all right. Calie's salad was amazing, filled with lettuce, celery, shredded radish, nuts and dried fruit.

"I don't follow a recipe," she said. "Just work by instinct."

"It's good," Alicia said. "Thank you."

"Also, it has all the antioxidants and minerals and vitamins that the pizza lacks." Calie was on her third slice.

"I'm with that," Alicia said. "But it's fabulous pizza, especially rustled up at short notice."

Brent shrugged. "I was going to have pizza for dinner anyway," he said with a wink.

And cringed at himself. Come on. This poor woman has had a terrible afternoon, she's miles from where she needs to be here you are coming on to her.

"Do you have pizza every night, then?" she said, and actually winked back.

"Well. I would hate to admit it, so I'll say mostly no. Mostly ramen. Ramen and salmon sandwiches."

"You sound like my dad. He would pretend like the five major food groups could all be found in a salmon sandwich. Fish, bread, butter and a couple of other things."

"Mayo and pepper," Calie said.

"Those were them."

There were more stories about fishing trips gone wrong and lost luggage and a stolen bicycle.

Alicia didn't offer much, but then that was to be expected. Calie was doing a great job of settling everyone's nerves.

By the end of the night, though, Calie had gotten started

on her third beer, which probably didn't put her near the limit, but Brent wasn't taking any chances and offered to drive her home.

"Then how do I get to work tomorrow."

"I'll swing by and pick you up."

Calie turned to Alicia. "You watch this one, hun'. He'll turn things around on you. Always with a solution."

Alicia was still only partway through her first beer. Brent liked that restraint. Plenty of people would have been powering through them like it was Spring Break.

"I'll watch him," Alicia said.

"Good girl." Calie patted her arm. "Whew. I'm not drunk, but I am a little heady. Maybe we should have dessert."

"Maybe we should call it a night," Brent said.

"You don't have ice cream?"

"I do, but I'm exhausted."

"With me?"

"Partly."

"Ouch. That hurts, you know? Tears me apart." Calie clutched at her sternum again.

"You're made of strong stuff," Brent said, standing. "You'll recover quickly."

"Of course I will."

"I'll be back in ten minutes," Brent told Alicia. "Feel free to tuck up and go to sleep if you need to. I'll just see you in the morning."

"Fine," Alicia said, standing with them.

Then Brent and Calie were out the front door and loading

up into his truck. When they got to Calie's place, Brent pulled right up into the driveway, by her front walk.

"Thanks," she said. "I mean it. Really thanks. Thanks for being a great boss. Thanks for bringing us through the emergency safely and efficiently. Thanks for pizza and good company."

"Thanks for coming." Calie made for a great buffer between himself and Alicia. Keeping the conversation going.

The attraction between them was clear, but the whole out-of-kilter nature of the situation made anything more just impossible.

Part of him hoped that she'd just gone to bed by the time he got back so that he wouldn't have to deal with any awkward moments before morning.

And then another part hoped she was still up. It wasn't late, and it would be a pleasant way to pass the rest of the evening, just talking with her. Exploring that palpable energy.

Even if it ultimately went nowhere.

"You know," Calie said, jerking his thoughts back to the car.

"I do know," he said.

"You don't even know what I was going to say."

"You were going to say that Alicia was a delight, and that I should make an effort, but still remain a gentleman."

"I don't know about the gentleman part. She looks like she's hungry for it."

"Goodnight Calie." Brent gestured toward her house.

"Ah, the hint." She opened the door and stepped out into the cool evening air. She leaned back in, watching him.

"What?" he said.

"You, my friend, let opportunity slip through your fingers like melting snow."

"As you said, I'm a gentleman."

"Yes." Calie gave a broad smile. "Yes you are. A little too much for your own good."

"Goodnight Calie."

"Goodnight Brent." Calie closed the door and walked steadily up to her front door. Brent waited until she had gotten the door open, given a little wave, and gone inside before backing out and heading home.

Nervous, which wasn't like him at all.

Still, tomorrow Alicia would be on a flight heading north and he would carry on with his life.

Perhaps wondering what might have happened had circumstances been a little different. But then, he had paperwork to do, and a fishing trip to plan, and spouting that needed a good clean out.

Chapter Seven

Alicia tidied up after the meal at Brent's place. Drying the dishes, there were a few things she couldn't find homes for so she just left them tidily on the table.

She wrapped the two leftover pieces of pizza in aluminum foil and put them on a shelf in the fridge. She put Saran wrap over the bowl of salad and placed it next to the foiled pizza.

It was so odd to be in a stranger's house, left alone with the dishes.

She didn't even know his family name.

In the spare room, she organized her things again and tucked away the documents. She couldn't stand to read them again.

She checked her phone and replied to messages from Olivia and Melissa and David. She marked herself safe on social media, then undid that. The plane had landed in one piece. Everyone was unhurt.

The incident wouldn't have even made the news beyond specialist sites and maybe some channel in Fairbanks if news was slow today.

Alicia lay on the bed and stretched out, still dressed. She was wired. Probably tomorrow it would hit her and she would be exhausted. Especially if she couldn't sleep.

And tomorrow would be the worst possible time to be fading out. She needed to be sharp to deal with everything.

Again, she cursed David for his lack of involvement.

She texted him again.

Since you won't be here tomorrow, keep your phone on you.

She sent it, then sent another.

Every second.

Sent that, then another.

Or I will come back to your place with a dump truck filled with Dad's stuff and just leave it on your lawn.

Sent.

She felt better now. Taking it out on David was entirely appropriate.

She'd brought along a paperback. One of the Stephen King wannabes that show up in airport bookstore racks all the time. She had read some on the plane and the story was all right. Engaging at least.

But now when she lay back on the bed and opened the book up to her marked spot, she couldn't even remember what had just happened.

As she flicked back a chapter, knowing that it was hopeless anyway, the front door opened. She hadn't even heard the truck pull up again.

Brent stepped in and kicked off his shoes just inside the front door. He looked in the spare room's doorway.

"Hey," he said. "Comfy? I figured you'd be asleep already."

"Too keyed up, really. I should go for a ten mile jog to clear my head and wear myself out."

"I'd come with," he said.

"Really? You run?"

"Sure."

"And box and push weights and work out on a rowing machine?"

"Well, kayak sometimes. Down on Earle River. There's a stretch about a mile and a half long that's flat, but fast. Paddle up it until I'm exhausted and then just paddle slowly back down. Among the ash and the birds and wildflowers."

"Sounds wonderful. You'll have to take me up there sometime."

Involuntarily, her eyes widened. Surprised at herself for saying that.

"I'd like to take you," Brent said.

"It's a date then." She managed a sideways smile. "Next time I'm in town."

"Next time." He stepped back from the door a fraction. "Anything you need?"

She held up the paperback. "I think I'm set. I'll read until I fall asleep. If I fall asleep."

"You need a pill?"

"You have pills?"

"No."

"You don't have trouble sleeping then."

"Nope."

"Me either. Usually."

"I get it today."

Alicia sat up. Put the book aside and swung her stocking feet onto the floor.

"You don't usually do this, do you? Have 'survivors' come and stay over."

"Nope. But then, mostly there aren't survivors." He gave a slight shake of his head. "That sounded wrong. Mostly there's no need. People already have a home to go to, or they get flown out to the hospital in Tronetown or maybe Fairbanks. We don't have this kind of thing very often. I mean, never before. There's a whole row of protocols happening around us now. The airline is hard at work, the airport is busy with the details. Tomorrow Calie and I will probably get pulled into a series of meetings and debriefings. There are bound to be things we could have done better."

"Like ensuring every last passenger had somewhere to stay."

"There you are."

She could smell him again. Clean and strong. A little bit of the cooking smell from the pizza.

She stood. Took a step toward him.

Brent. He was quite the specimen. The right height. She would have to tip her head up to kiss him, and he would have to tip down, but then, it was like that with most guys she'd dated.

All three of them.

Well, that guy Len back in college didn't count. Not really. Just a couple of times, fumbling and bumbling. And he had been a little shorter, so kissing him had been almost eye to eye.

Why was she even thinking about that?

"You have a look in your eye," Brent said.

"I do?" She smiled. "What kind of a look?"

"Thoughtful. Wistful. Allur..."

"Alluring?" she said. Good grief, he was attracted to her.

And now they were alone in his house.

In a bedroom.

She felt herself trembling.

Think straight girl. This is no way to get over the shock of the little adventure aboard the broken airplane. A good sleep is what is needed.

"Alluring, yes," he said, stepping back. "Sorry." He glanced off along the hallway. "I've enjoyed your company. I'm sorry it's been under forced circumstances."

He took another step back.

Don't go. Stay there. Let me look at you. Let me dissolve in your eyes.

"Yes," she said. "Forced circumstances. It was a good thing." She found herself taking a step back too. Sensible.

"Good?"

"Well, I would have flown right on over. Landed on time in Candleton. Right now I would be up at my father's place, despairing. Sad. But instead now I've gotten to take a little forced break. Gotten to dine with some fine people."

Brent smiled. And nodded. He seemed to consider something.

She stared into his eyes, and she could see it right there. He wanted to kiss her.

Was the attraction between them strong that it was just in the air. Like that?

He swallowed.

She stepped closer again. Their eyes were firmly locked on each other. His breathing was measured and even. He had the slightest of smiles.

"Perhaps after I'm done up in Candleton," she said, "I could come back for a few days. You could take me kayaking."

Very sensible. Her mother would be proud, but Alicia could still hear Olivia's voice chiding her. *Jump him, girl,* Olivia would say. *Just jump him now.*

"Kayaking?" Brent said. "Yeah. That would be nice."

"Sleep well."

"Well you too."

He gave her another sweet wink and strode off along the hallway.

He was just so tempting. It was an awful long g time since she'd felt anything like this. A kind of animal lust that would burst upon her during her twenties.

She closed the door and leaned back against it.

"Whew," she whispered. "Olivia, you are a bad influence."

Chapter Eight

Brent's head swirled for a moment when he lay back on his pillow. He'd actually changed his sheets and pillowslips a couple of days back and they still felt fresh and crisp. Comfy. Welcoming.

Alone.

And it felt worse with someone else in the house. Let alone an attractive, sharp woman.

He sighed and smiled to himself. The two bedrooms were on the same side of the house, but the bathroom lay between them. It was a standard layout that probably half the houses in Wilkes Landing had.

Half the houses in back blocks Alaska.

It was probably just as well she was going in the morning. Otherwise he would make a fool of himself. Even with Calie's expert guidance.

The idea of kayaking with Alicia in a few days was a nice

thought, but wildly improbable. Of course. She'd just said it to kind of make it feel a little more open. As if there was more possibility there.

The poor woman probably just needed to get to sleep so she could at least do the best she could when she finally arrived in Candleton.

Brent felt for her, that was for sure. Not necessarily estranged from her father, but it was clear they'd been distant. And her brother wasn't being any help.

It must have all been quite surreal for her already, without tossing in the sudden landing in a strange town.

A pity, really. Other circumstances and he would have enjoyed getting to know her. Kayaking and coffee and dumb jokes.

Probably he wouldn't even louse it up.

He slept, deeply, with just a couple of vague and fleeting dreams about the aircraft's engine fire spreading.

But he woke refreshed. The spare room door was closed, so he showered again and started in on breakfast. Eggs, bacon and toast.

As the bacon sizzled, filling the house with the delicious aroma, Brent's phone rang. Calie.

"You're awake already?" he said.

"Talking to you, aren't I? Anyway, I barely slept. So here's the plan. There's no other aircraft around with the capacity to take all the passengers on to Candleton. They've rustled up a couple of six-seaters, but then it's getting back into helicopters and the airline is reluctant to stump up for those. They've had a bad year, apparently."

"The plane wasn't even full."

"I know it."

"But how do you know all these details already? It's barely even seven in the AM."

"Brent. Have you heard of 'the internet'. It's magical."

"Magical, huh?"

"I ask it questions and it gives me the answers."

"Who'd have thought?"

"So yeah, I've been keeping myself in the loop on it all. Official-like. People from the airline have been up all night working on things. There's not just the passengers, there's the plane itself, and the investigators, and getting engineers to actually fix the thing. Then there are other people in Candleton who would themselves like to become passengers tomorrow, but that's not happening. The airline has four planes, that's it. All scheduled for other things. They don't have the luxury of a big buffer between them and disaster."

"I can imagine."

"Anyway, here's my idea. Why don't you offer to drive Alicia to Candleton. Then she—"

"It's a couple hundred miles, right?"

"So I heard, but there are short cuts. And the roads are really good. Especially this time of year."

"If there were short cuts they would just be the route. And the roads are lousy. The trucks tear them apart and the ice and just the whole landscape in general."

"Quit whining. How did it go with her last night?"

"How do you mean?"

"Did the two of you stay up all night talking? I could see

that between you. That energy. You probably got less sleep than me."

"When I got home we said goodnight and went to bed. In our own beds."

"Oh how dull. Clearly my skills are fading."

"Perhaps you're focusing on the wrong skillset."

"Oh you are a riot."

From the hallway came the sound of the spare room door opening. Alicia appeared a moment later in the kitchen doorway.

Her hair was a tousled mess and she was wearing the Coldplay shirt again. No bra, he noticed, and quickly made sure to bring his eyes back to hers.

The towel was wrapped around her waist.

"Going to take a shower," she said. "If that's all right. Still feel grimy."

"Of course," he said. "Go ahead. Remember to watch that mixer."

"Jumps from 'Alaskan Lake' to 'Hawaiian Volcano' at around seven o'clock."

He grinned. "You got it."

She smiled back. Lingered a moment. Then headed off along the hall in a swirl of vague sleep scent.

"Hello?" Calie said. "Are you still there, boss?"

"Still here." Brent turned to check the bacon. Just a little too well done. He slipped it off the pan and onto the waiting plates.

"So that's your new girlfriend you were gawping at, huh?" Calie said.

"So wrong that you would say that," he said. "On so many levels."

"I know, but that's why you keep me around. Hey, listen I'm going to walk over and pick up my Jeep soon. Thanks for driving me home."

"Welcome."

"When I show up, I'll poke my head in. So long as I won't be interrupting anything."

"Just breakfast. You want to join?"

"Oh! I would love to, but there's this part of me that's thinking that you are looking for a little air-gap between you and your new lady-love. Just so that things don't get too steamy before you have to drive her up to Candleton."

"You really don't let up, do you?"

"Me? No. This is what makes me an excellent emergency responder."

"I know. Better get over here soon, your bacon's going to get crisped to charcoal."

"Oh, I love it like that."

"See you soon."

Chapter Nine

Alicia dried off and dressed again, conscious of Brent's roving eyes. She was used it that, from men, but on him it was different. Probably just because she liked him.

How about that? She liked him. Even after a good night's sleep. She noticed that she was no longer trembling. No longer having thoughts of fiery catastrophic ground impact whirling in her mind.

She was calm. In Alaska, and north of Juneau, so that was something.

Almost within reach of Candleton.

They had a delicious breakfast, with Calie's chatty, delightful company keeping things alive. People like her and Brent made it tempting to toss in Tulsa and move to this part of the world.

Perhaps that was what had been up with her father shifting his whole life up this way.

She knew so little of the background to that.

Brent made them coffees in insulated carry cups, using soy milk in hers. He had a carton in his cupboard, which was pretty impressive.

Then they were back up at the airport. Already some of the other passengers from yesterday were there. The place was bustling with locals, some official, some just plain dropping by for the gossip value, but to help as well. The Alaskan way. The Wilkes Landing way.

Things moved quickly. Well-organized. A couple more planes came in and Brent assisted with loading them up. The passengers were clearly nervous. Their last flight had involved flames, and emergency responses and a night in a strange town.

People were prioritized. A single woman traveling without family fell down the list. Of course. She could accept that. Calie had been over it at breakfast.

But there was always the chance that something else might show up. Calie had said that she might have gotten it wrong.

Besides, the airline's official representatives wanted to offer their apologies, and to keep it all straight. No one wanted to be sued, of course.

Then the first aircraft was gone, and the second one was landing on the long strip of tarmac. People bustled and someone from town showed up with an enormous box filled with sandwiches, and a cooler filled with sodas.

Lunchtime, and Alicia had barely even registered.

She'd spent a half an hour on the phone with Olivia, answering every question. Was she hurt? Where had she stayed? What kind of compensation was the airline offering?

Then Olivia was onto her own issues, about her husband Greg and his secretary, about little Marcy's problems at pre-school and Linden's achievements at elementary.

When Olivia moved on to all the new updates on who was doinking whom in their wider group, Alicia knew it was time to end the call.

"Got to go," she said. "Things are happening here."

"Keep me up to date."

"Of course."

Thankfully Olivia hadn't asked about whether Alicia had met any hot fire fighters.

She called David and their conversation took all of a minute and a half. He asked if she was all right, and told her to take care. To give him a call when she got to the house.

"I am interested," he said. "Just the timing is bad."

"It's unlikely that the timing of a parent's death will ever be convenient."

"Sure. Just throw out anything you can't sell right away. I could mail you a box of matches for the bonfire."

Melissa's phone went to voice mail.

Then, the call she was dreading.

To Howie. Her manager at Brealdon and Partners. Roading and housing development brokers. Alicia was one of the best with the contracts, and at negotiating with clients.

Not *one of* the best, though. The *actual* best.

And she was going to have to tell him that she would be away at least an extra day.

Already he had shown remarkably little sympathy. He'd never gotten along with his parents. He'd been disappointed when they'd moved from Maine to Florida a couple of years back.

"Less chance of winter killing them," he'd said to Alicia at the time.

"Maybe a better excuse to visit them," she'd said. "Take a coral cruise and go to a couple of theme parks."

"See, that makes it sound even worse."

The guy would make the Grinch seem positively joyous. But he paid well, and because he had interests across five states she got to be out the office and away from him a good third of the time.

He picked up on the third ring. Tulsa was hours ahead. It was already nearing mid-afternoon.

"Dramatic," he said when she told him about the plane. "I suppose this means you want more time."

"I've lost a day on the estate already," she said. "And it's looking as if I won't get on another flight today."

"The Glass and Wilbur contract is moving ahead. They want to sign tomorrow, but I want your eyes over some of the clauses they've deleted."

Alicia sighed. Bereavement was supposed to mean your brain couldn't be expected to be on the job.

"Email it to me," she said. "I'll get it back to you within an hour."

"That sure would be appreciated."

"Assuming I have a connection," she added. "If I'm in the air or..." She glanced at Brent. "... or on the road, then I may be a little delayed."

"Today," he said. "Just to have it done today would be appreciated."

"I know it. And I know you'll show your appreciation too."

"I will, I will." Howie knew that he was lucky to have Alicia on his team. The appreciation might be tickets to a game or a concert, or maybe a voucher for one of the local electrical stores where he cultivated friends among the managers.

Never, though, an extra few days to manage her father's estate. To Howie, work was everything, and appreciation came by way of real world things. Not anything involving an emotion of any kind.

"All right," she said, still watching Brent. "We'll talk soon."

"Soon. Great. Thanks." Howie rang off.

Brent was near the front of the terminal building, by the doors, talking with a man in jeans and a sports jacket. Probably the airport manager.

Alicia made her way over. The remaining passengers and locals still milled around. Quiet conversations murmured through the space. The big clock ticked on and the small clocks led or followed. The second hands were out of sync.

"Alicia," Brent said as Alicia came up, "this is Red Dalton. He's in charge of the airport here. Red, Alicia."

Alicia held out her hand. "Pleased to meet you. Sorry for all the trouble with the plane."

"Goodness me," Red said. "Ain't none of your fault at all. That was the plane."

"I know it. But still, a nuisance for all concerned."

"Well I'm thankful that you all got off safely. Little bit of damage to some airplane doesn't matter squat if the passengers are safe."

"I agree, of course."

Red smiled. "Brent tells me that he's taking you through to Candleton later today."

"That was his kind offer, but I wouldn't want to keep him away from the airport when he's needed."

"I think we've got it," Red said. "Brent and Calie and the team have done the job and all that's left now is paperwork. Things are gratefully under control now."

Red looked around the terminal. People were sipping at coffees and nibbling on sandwiches. There was a little tension in the air, but nothing like there had been the previous day.

Alicia was actually feeling good. Perhaps a drive north wouldn't be so bad.

A tingle ran through her as she realized that it would mean spending hours in his company.

On one hand, that sounded simply wonderful. On the other hand it was almost as terrifying as looking out an aircraft window and seeing the engine on fire.

She smiled at herself. The engine hadn't been *on fire*. It had been smoking and sparking and *threatening* to catch alight. Would that be something that happened over time? The story growing and the drama of it all increasing?

"How long do you think it will take to get to Candleton?" she said. "A couple of hours?"

"Three," Brent said. "At least. Certainly under four. It's a while since I've been up that way."

Four hours.

"You better get started," Red said. "If Brent's going to get back before dark."

"Well, he could..." Alicia trailed off. Had she been about to offer that he could stay the night and come back in the morning? On a level that seemed more than fair, after all he'd welcomed her into his home. And her father's place had plenty of space.

And it would be weird to be there alone. Kicking around in a big old dark house.

Both Brent and Red were staring at her.

"Sorry," Alicia said, flustered. "Opening my mouth before a thought was fully formed. I would assume that driving in the dark would be no issue for someone like you anyway." That just came out badly. Really she should just get out on the road with her thumb and hitch her way north.

"Driving in the dark is fine," Brent said. "No issue at all."

"But still," Red said. "You kids should get underway really. Grab a coffee and hit the road."

Kids? Both she and Brent were in their thirties, and Red couldn't have been beyond mid fifties.

"You're a sweet man, Red," Alicia said, unsure why she'd said it. Perhaps she could still trade a little on the trauma of the previous day to say goofy things.

He touched her arm. "I'm just so glad that everyone's safe.

Now, you two, get going. I've got a thousand things to organize and most of those are ducks not in a row." He shook Brent's hand and then Alicia's.

"Thanks boss," Brent said.

"Well, thank *you*. Alaska could use more men of your ilk, let me say."

"Go organize your ducks," Brent said. "I'll drop Alicia safely to Candleton, and see you tomorrow."

"Thanks, thanks, thanks." Red shook Alicia's hand too, then headed away into the throng.

Alicia looked at Brent and said, "He's more like a politician than an airport manager."

"He's also the deputy mayor," Brent said.

"Can I pick 'em or what?"

Brent smiled.

Alicia sighed at her apparently increasing capacity to make goofy comments. *Can I pick 'em.* What did that even mean?

"Sufficiently caffeinated?" he said. "Hungry? You might want to grab a sandwich. There's not a whole lot between here and Candleton."

"I'm fine," she said. "Let's get underway."

Chapter Ten

The road was good and clear. There had been some early snowfalls, but nothing serious yet. Brent didn't need the truck's plough and, like all good Alaskans, he'd checked the forecast before departing. Even though the forecasts could be wildly wrong and subject to hourly updates. Updates that could change things a hundred and eighty degrees.

And there were always localized variations. Pockets were snow never fell, and other pockets where it never melted. Parts of the road where the wind could tip over a bulldozer, and other parts where wildflowers grew lush and verdant as if they were on a Hawaiian mountainside.

He loved it out here.

The truck hummed along, it's engine just purring and the tires grumbling along the tarmac. There were so many sections where the bitumen had been cut out and replaced.

Potholes filled only to develop new potholes around, which had themselves been filled. Patches on patches on patches.

Calie would tell him that there were some sections that had none of the original-laid road surface left, and were entirely made of patches. It didn't surprise him.

Alicia sat beside him, quiet. Looking at her phone from time to time. Looking out the windows mostly.

Ten miles slipped by in silence. Normally that wouldn't bother him a bit. Plenty of his friends were not big talkers.

He'd done entire drives out to Fendalville and Lake Maguire with Tobes and Josh where no one had spoken for close to two hours. The first thing anyone said would have been when they got to the boat ramp and Brent started backing the truck around and Josh would say, "Left hand down a bit."

But right now it felt different. How often did he get the chance to spend hours like this with a gorgeous, amazing woman?

Whoops. Where did that come from? He'd been attracted to her from the get-go, but *gorgeous* and *amazing*? Just popping into his head unbidden.

What was behind that?

Perhaps it was a good thing. He was enjoying her quiet energy.

Just as well Calie wasn't with them.

"Up here a ways," Brent said, "there's a nice spot. Uranium Point. The road rises and there's a great view across the valley."

Mostly they were just driving through the stands of plantation pine. Big trees nearing maturity. Sometime in the next five or so years, someone would come through with chainsaws and take the trees down. Then would come the trucks and the logs would get hauled away. After that, work crews would stride along with pine seedlings and plant them in neat rows, just a few yards apart.

Heading for harvesting thirty or forty years hence.

"Uranium Point," Alicia said. "Sounds pretty."

Sarcastic? Well, of course.

"It is pretty," he said. "The name makes no sense. Maybe once upon a time someone had big plans for a mine out here?"

"Or a power station."

"Maybe."

"Or perhaps they just have a sense of humor. I bet there's an Abattoir Lookout and a Salted Caramel Grove."

"Hey! I like salted caramel."

"Really? I never got it. Caramel is delicious. Sweet. Why put salt on it? You put salt on pork or fries."

"Sure, but it's a really versatile mineral. I kind of picked you for salted caramel latte kind of woman."

"More like pumpkin spice." She grinned. Playful. He liked that.

"There you are. A pumpkin spice latte with soy and a sprinkle of cinnamon on your way to a deposition."

"I'm kidding. Black coffee is just fine with me. And I'm not a lawyer, so I don't do depositions."

"You do contracts, though."

"I do. The legal people look them over and make sure that it's all in order. What I'm good at is negotiating with the clients, and explaining it. The lawyers get themselves tangled up, so I'm the person they send into the fray."

Brent smiled over at her.

"What?" she said.

"Oh, just that most people I know are too self-effacing to ever say that they are good at something."

"Do you think I should be more humble?"

"I think you should be exactly who you are."

Brent slowed and pulled in by the Uranium Point sign.

The raised area looked out over the braided shingle of the Marbolly River. There were small groves or solitary trees on some of the islands, and trees all along the far bank, marking the edge of the start of thick and endless forest that rolled across the hills like dark green icing.

The lookout was just gravel, with a few wooden posts driven in, standing about a foot high, to discourage unfortunate events with vehicles driving over the edge. There was an overflowing trash can, and a beaten up sign with a map of the area.

"It's beautiful," Alicia said, leaning forward to look out over the wide, low valley.

Brent reached to the truck's central console, where they'd both set their coffees in the cupholders. He took his and sipped. It was growing a little cool, so he had a good slug of it.

Alicia took hers too.

"The shadows are already growing," she said. "It must be strange living in a place where the sun is always so far south."

"I grew up here, so actually I think I would find it weird to be in Oklahoma where the sun gets directly overhead."

"Never that high. Sometimes, maybe in June it feels that way, but we're still a long way north of the Tropic of Cancer so I... what?"

"What, what?"

She stared at him. Her eyes were just so delicious. So blue and intense. Her pupils were small, as if she was laser-focused on him.

"I mean why are you looking at me like that?" she said.

Because I want to kiss you.

"Because not many people talk about the Tropics," he said.

The Tropic of Capricorn, in the south, and the Tropic of Cancer, in the north, were the two lines that paralleled the equator and marked the southern and northern-most reaches where the sun was ever directly overhead. June for the Tropic of Cancer and December for the Tropic of Capricorn.

Like the Arctic Circle and the Antarctic circle, which marked the lines beyond which there would be at least one twenty-four hour period each year where the sun stayed below the horizon. Then on to the poles, where it stayed below for six months.

"I know about them on account of my father," Alicia said. She took another sip from her coffee and set it back in the holder. "Living up here, he's not far from the Arctic Circle, so we used to talk about the long days or the long nights."

"Pretty harsh environments out that way. Extremes and fast changes."

"Do you think it's not like that down here?" Was she leaning a little closer to him?

He could smell her. Clean, but with a half a day of waiting around on her. Sweet and alluring.

He stayed focused on her eyes.

Could he be misreading this?

Probably.

Calie would tell him no. Tell him to just go ahead and kiss her.

What would you lose? He could hear Calie's voice. *Either she kisses back or she pulls away. If she does the latter, then just drive on in silence. Should be easy for you. Drop her off and come on home.*

"I think it is like that down here," Alicia said. Her eyes stayed locked right on him.

"Long days in the summer," he said, feeling odd. His heart rate had definitely come up.

How could that be? She was just someone who'd flown in. Landed in the wrong place.

But boy was she attractive. Her sultry voice, her fabulous eyes, her thick hair.

And the way she talked. Assertive and strong.

Plenty of strong women in Alaska. Calie's voice.

But it was true.

"Long nights in winter," Alicia said, with a slight skewing to her smile. As if she was being wicked.

"Long nights," he said. "Stay indoors and wrap up warm."

"Sounds..." She trailed off. "Brent."

"Alicia?"

"I just..." She took a breath and pursed her lips. She put both hands up to her face and blew through them. "Sorry, just calming my nerves."

"Nerves?" he said. Good grief, he was sure experiencing that right now. Was he reading this right?

So many times he hadn't.

What would you lose?

He leaned forward.

From behind the truck came the blast of a horn.

The crackle of tires on gravel.

Brent jerked upright. Grabbed the steering wheel.

Colors flashed in the mirrors.

The hiss and clatter of engine brakes. The rumble of the engine itself.

A semi.

Then the truck had gone on by. Sweeping around the bend and vanishing back off in the direction of Wilkes Landing.

Brent's adrenalin surge tingled away.

"Taking the corner too fast," he said. The truck must have come off the tarmac a little. Gone onto the viewpoint parking lot's gravel.

But stayed under control.

Sped away. A schedule to keep.

"That was close," he said.

Alicia was adjusting the shoulders of her shirt.

Staring through the back window.

"Yes," she said, and flicked her eyes to him. "Very close."

Brent started the truck and they drove on.

Chapter Eleven

Alicia used her phone's maps to guide Brent through the darkening streets of Candleton. It was after four in the afternoon already. It had taken hours to drive through the endless stands of thick trees.

Water lay on the road, making the streetlights glisten back at her.

"Left up here," she said.

Her father's place was on Bondurant Street, which was filled with big old two story villas with wide, homey verandas and tall trees in the yards. Could have just about been a neighborhood in suburban Tulsa.

Brent pulled up right out front and Alicia found she couldn't look.

Not at Brent.

Not at the house.

The drive had been quiet. For the most part.

Neither of them had said much.

Even so, she felt as if she knew him.

Right back there at Uranium Point, they'd had a close call.

They hadn't talked about it at all. Not the truck. Not the obvious physical attraction.

Clearly she was emotional. Coming to the house where her father had died.

The call had come early in the morning. David. The local coroner had called him. But the night before. It had been eight at night in Alaska when one of the neighbors had called the paramedics, after eleven by the time Nathan Brooks's death certificate had been signed. The early hours of the morning in Oklahoma.

"I called," David had said, "but I got voicemail."

"And you didn't think to leave a message?" she'd said. Angry. Hurt. Devastated.

"No," he'd said. "Is that how you'd want to find out? A message? Best just to speak to you directly."

Alicia had to admit that he was right.

"How are you doing?" Brent said now, jerking her back to the fading light of the Alaskan evening. Light played through the houses. The air smelled of smoke.

"Me?" she said, remembering the documents the city had sent. Candleton wanted to develop the land here. Knock down six old houses and put up a condominium.

You would think that she would know how to handle developments like that. But it was too close to home. She was doing the best to put it out of her mind.

"Lots on your mind," Brent said. "More than just your father's death."

A chill ran through her. More than just from the rapidly cooling air. Not many people were that straightforward. There were so many platitudes. Moved on. Passed away. Loss.

But death was what it was. Her father was dead.

"We should have eaten," she said, feeling both suddenly hungry, and suddenly unwilling to go indoors. Into his house. "Is there a place we can get some fries or something? A burger?"

"Probably. I haven't been up this way much." He was watching her with those intense eyes.

Without saying anything more, he started the truck and pulled away from the curb. He made a U-turn and headed back toward the town center.

There was a town square with a courthouse with white pillars and wide steps. A few parked pickups and numerous people out walking.

Two pickups were parked door to door, facing opposite ways in the center of the street. The drivers had their windows down and were talking, oblivious to anything else.

"It's all so slow," Alicia said.

"Really?" Brent said. "It feels busy to me."

He nosed up behind one of the pickups and stopped a moment. The drivers called out their farewells drove off. The one coming toward them lifted his arm and waved. Thick glasses and a Stetson and a wide grin.

Across the square from the courthouse, Alicia spotted a café with flapping banners and a carving of an upright bear chain sawed in wood. When Brent parked out front, they saw a chalkboard sign reading *Our Specialty? Everything!* and inside it reflected that. Milkshake flavors and a top shelf of spirits.

A coffee machine, a cabinet with bagels, Danishes and croissants, another with sausages and cuts of meat and cheese and salads. Like a deli.

"What do you think?" Brent said, clearly at home. Alicia was feeling overwhelmed, right when she needed simplicity.

The smells, though, were just wonderful. Almost strong enough that she could gather all her nutritional requirements just from the air.

The board on the wall behind the counters had about as much information at the flight schedule displays in a big airport. Burgers and fries, Chinese meals, pizza, subs, steak and vegetables.

The list of beverages was longer than some of the lists in her contracts.

"Just a flat white," she whispered.

"You want a cookie too?" He pointed to a part of one of the cabinets with fat, oversized cookies filled with chocolate chips, nuts and dried fruit. Some even had icing.

Clearly this was the place to be in Candleton. Of the dozen tables, only a couple were unoccupied, and two wait-staff bustled.

"A cookie?" Brent said.

"Sure. You choose. I'll go find a seat before the place fills up completely." From her jeans pocket she took her little wallet and slipped out a twenty. She held it out to him.

Brent held his hand up. "It's fine. I've got it."

"I insist. You've driven me up here. I owe you."

"Really, it's fine. All part of the service."

"Take the money," she said. "There's a distinct line between chivalry and chauvinism."

"Hey, what? Where did that come from?"

"Let me buy you a coffee. I'm not some maiden in distress who needs you pandering to her."

The briefest of scowls crossed his face.

What was going on with her? This guy liked her, for goodness sake and here she was getting all haughty with him.

But then he took the twenty.

"No trouble," he said, then waved it almost in her face. "Thanks."

Alicia turned and looked for a table. One near the door had just emptied and a pretty young ginger-haired waitress was wiping the table down.

"Thanks," Alicia said, slipping by her and sitting.

"You ordered?" the young woman said. Her name badge read *Cheyenne*. Pretty name too.

"My driver is ordering for me."

"Driver, huh? Fancy."

"No, I didn't mean it like that. It's just... well I don't know how to describe him."

Cheyenne looked around. "Boyfriend?" she said, looking back at Alicia. "Fiancé?"

"I was on the plane that made an emergency landing on its way up here," Alicia said. "He was one of the fire crew and he offered to bring me up here."

"Omigosh, he's a fire fighter too. Don't let him out of your sight."

"I'm sure there a plenty of fire fighters in Alaska."

"Gay, married, dimwits." Cheyenne counted off on her fingers. "I guess he's one of those, huh?"

"No."

Cheyenne smiled and winked. It was as if she was in league with Calie.

"You're in town for a while?" Cheyenne said.

Alicia looked around the café. Surely Cheyenne should be working the tables rather than gossiping.

"Oh, it's fine," Cheyenne said. "This ain't like New York."

"Pace of life, huh?"

"You bet."

"Right. Not like Tulsa, either."

"You're from Tulsa? Um?" Cheyenne screwed her face up momentarily. "Oklahoma."

"That's the one."

"Well, Oklahoma's a lot like Alaska, really."

"Nothing's like Alaska."

"You've got the snow, you've got the beautiful mountains."

Alicia smiled. "I suppose so."

"You've got Texas to contend with, and we've got Canada."

"Different worlds."

"Exactly! Of course, we've got crab fishing and forestry and mining and oil."

"And we've got corn farming."

"Wow." Another cute Cheyenne wink. "Not so alike after all. Here comes your beau. Isn't that what you said?"

Brent was striding back from the counter

"Driver," Alicia said.

"That's the word. I guess I'll be right back with whatever you ordered."

"Thank you."

Another wink, and Cheyenne was off. She stopped a couple of tables along and began charming the customers there too.

"Flat white coming up," Brent said, pulling out the seat opposite and sitting. He set down a small engraved piece of glass on a stand, with a number. *22.*

As if Cheyenne might need guiding to the correct table.

Around the café walls were small framed photographs of wild lakes and craggy mountains. One, as if specifically to juxtapose, was of a tanned surfer on tall wave.

"Thanks," Alicia said. "I appreciate you giving me a moment."

"It must be tough. Coming home like this."

"It was never home."

"Sorry, I meant to your father's home. His actual house."

Alicia didn't reply.

Brent rolled his shoulders. He was just really easing himself out after hours on the road, but it was an attractive movement. Did he know that?

"You don't have to wait around," she said. "You probably want to get on the road. I could grab my bag and just walk up when I feel ready."

"That wouldn't be very gentlemanly would it? Besides, a

break here is good. Halfway. Before I turn around and whistle my way back home."

She would miss him. How odd was that. Her transfer in Juneau had been surprisingly quick. Less than an hour on the ground. Most of what she'd seen of Alaska had been with this man.

Now he was about to leave and make his way back home. Back to his little house and his life of fire fighting and fishing and watching the game.

They'd talked a whole lot last night. About nothing, really. Family and hobbies and trying to be adults in a world that had certain boxes for what adults should be. Married in your mid-twenties, second child before thirty, mortgage under control before your mid-forties.

Neither of them were really fitting the mold.

What would it be like to move up here and be with him?

Alicia leaned back in her seat and stared at the ceiling.

"What?" he said. "Did I say something wrong?"

How could she answer that? That somewhere in the mess that was her head, she was thinking with lust rather than any vague kind of practicality?

She had her father's estate to organize. A job back in Tulsa. A *good* job, even if her boss could be a bit of a putz.

"Nothing wrong," Alicia said, looking back again into Brent's intense eyes. They were just captivating. "Emotional turmoil, perhaps. Here I am in Candleton, just down the road from where he lived out his last years. I don't even know what kind of a life he had up here. Add to that the fact that I don't even know what kind of man he became after he pushed us away."

"Also the whole way you've arrived here."

"Right. As if the universe was trying to tell me to stay away from Candleton."

A close call with the aircraft. A close call with a truck, coinciding with a close call with Brent's perfect lips and brilliantly structured musculature.

Whew. She really needed to get a grip.

He was smiling at her.

Right then Cheyenne arrived with two coffees in cups and saucer, and a bread and butter plate with two fat, iced cookies.

"You two enjoy that," she said. "Welcome to Candleton."

"Thanks," Brent said with a warm smile.

A startling worm of jealousy went around Alicia's heart. As if he was flirting with Cheyenne, and should have been keeping all of his attention on Alicia.

Silly. Why was she feeling this way. She'd never experienced this kind of thing with a man before. Certainly not a man she'd met little more than twenty-four hours earlier.

Well, not met, technically. That moment they'd shared on the tarmac, the electrical eye contact, didn't count as meeting someone.

Cheyenne wafted away, stopping again at another table to make conversation.

"She's cute," Alicia said, without meaning to. "Good at her job."

"I guess," Brent said, all eyes for Alicia now. He picked up his coffee and sipped.

The cookies lay there, tempting. Not good for her really.

"Pistachio," he said, pointing to the lighter one. "And chocolate-chocolate chip. With chocolate icing and chocolate sprinkles."

Heavenly.

"Do you want to split them?" Alicia took a knife from the caddy in the middle of the table.

"You cut, I choose?" he said.

"What are you, six?"

"Going on seven." His grin was infectious and Alicia found herself grinning back.

Around her the quiet murmurs of the café faded even more into the background.

She cut, and Brent chose. She'd intentionally made the choice obvious, and he took the smaller of the chocolate cookie pieces, and she took the smaller of the pistachio pieces.

Oh, boy, it was just heavenly. The first bite practically turned to sweet, crisp melted butter in her mouth. The taste was extraordinary. As if the pistachios grew on a tree out back and had just been picked right before the cookie had been baked.

"That good, huh?" Brent said.

"What?" Alicia said through the soft crumbs.

"The look on your face. I thought you were... well. Enjoying it very much."

She just about choked.

"I was," she said. "I was enjoying it very much. How about you with your little sliver of chocolate there?"

Brent swallowed.

"Well," he said. "It's sticky and warm. Soft to the touch. Tastes just right. A mix of sweet and bitter. A little testy at times, but then it's had a tough day."

She didn't know whether to scowl at him, or smile.

"Excuse me," he said. "It's good. I wish I'd taken the bigger piece."

"That's mine, buster. You keep your hands off it." Alicia set down the piece of pistachio and took a sip from her coffee.

The time passed with almost idle chitchat then, as if both of them wanted to keep back from any kind of vague, or less-than-vague, innuendo.

Alicia left a tip and Brent drove her back up to Bondurant Street.

One of the neighboring houses, just two along from her father's place had no fences and no trees. A notice tacked on the door. Had someone been evicted?

Brent parked and they got out and this time Alicia made it as far as the front door before she had to gather herself.

"You don't have a key?" Brent said, back on the second step up to the veranda.

"I have a key. That was one of Dad's things. That we would always have a key to his house. Each time he moved, a key would show up in the mail." Alicia took the little silvery

Yale key from her purse. The key slid right into the lubricated lock with a series of tiny clicks.

Alicia found herself standing there, finger and thumb gripping the key. Not quite ready to turn it.

Brent, bless him, didn't speak. He just stood behind her. Waiting.

Alicia dropped her hand and turned to him.

"It keeps getting later," she said. "And that road is really icy. You could stay here the night." She glanced at the door, realizing that she had no idea what she was going to find inside. Perhaps there were no beds.

Or perhaps just one bed.

No going back now.

"The road's not so icy," he said. "I've driven over it with a foot of snow, so—"

"A foot of snow?"

"I have the plough."

"You're a real Alaskan man, aren't you?"

He gave a wry smile. "Last time I checked."

And she gave a half-smile. Everything she said seemed to come out just a little wrong.

"I owe you," she said. "You drove me over. You had me stay at your place last night."

"You paid for the coffees and cookies. I call that even."

"Oh."

"But still, I'm not sure you should be going in here alone. You seem a little... tentative."

Terrified would be a better word, but tentative covered it too.

"Yes. I guess it could be like ripping off a Band-Aid, right?"

"Could be."

Alicia turned and took the key. She turned it. Turned the door handle.

Pushed the door open.

Chapter Twelve

A rich, thick stink washed over Brent on the veranda of Alicia's father's place. The wash of stale air that's been enclosed for too long. Of damp laundry and wallpaper glue and fruit and flowers that have been left sitting for weeks.

He could picture it all. Right there. Oranges and mandarins in a bowl. A vase of dead hydrangeas. Brushed cotton shirts and jeans in a laundry hamper. Rolls of wallpaper ready to hang, with a water bucket ready to activate the glue.

Who even still hung wallpaper? He wouldn't have even picked the smell except for a paramedic call out a few weeks back where Daisy Middelon, aged ninety-six, had fallen from a stool as she worked on re-papering her hallway.

"Whew," Alicia said. "What hey?"

"Yep," Brent said.

"First job is to go around and open up all the windows."

"Might be a bit buggy right now for that."

"Buggy? Here? The place is an ice cube. How can there be bugs?"

"Believe me, there are bugs."

"Have you people never heard of screens?"

"Sure, but I don't see any."

Alicia sighed.

"It's fine." Brent stepped up to her. "We can work it out."

She still didn't move. She just stood there staring into her father's house.

Behind her, Brent stayed silent. There was no rush. Things like this needed to unfold in their own time.

From one of the nearby houses came a sudden burst of laughter. Family time. People settling in for the evening. From farther off came the a dog's bark.

"Steeling myself," Alicia whispered.

Brent just kept quiet. No rush. Besides, there was nothing to say.

In the gloom of the house's interior, he could make out a stairway on the right and a hallway leading on through on the left. Thin light shone through, presumably from the kitchen at the back of the house. A tall end table stood near the door and along the lower side of the stairs, a cupboard stood ajar.

Kind of creepy, almost. Like teenagers in one of those movies where they are daring each other to go into the basement.

After another moment, Alicia took the step across the threshold into the house. She reached out to her right and flicked on a light.

Right away the house's interior transformed. Bright colors on the carpet and on some paintings on the walls. The thick, dark mahogany color of the staircase banister. The subtle, soft light floral patterns of the wallpaper.

Alicia stopped after a couple of steps.

Her shoulders rose and fell as she took slow, deep breaths.

He couldn't know exactly what she was thinking, but he stayed quiet. No need to intrude.

"Walk with me," she said. "I'm going to take a look around. Familiarize myself."

Brent followed her to the right, through at door at the base of the staircase. Again Alicia flicked a switch, drenching the room in stark white-yellow light. A living room, with an old sofa, a wooden coffee table, television, bookshelf, another bright painting on the wall. A print of that old Hockney image of someone diving into a stark swimming pool.

On the back wall stood a fireplace, with coals and ashes and a long mantle. A few pieces of polished wooden fruit stood on it, in a turned wooden bowl.

Above was a pair of impressive antlers mounted on a wooden shield.

"Hunter?" Brent said.

"Not that I know of. Maybe there were things I never knew about him."

"Isn't it the way?"

"Isn't it?"

There was another door beside the fireplace, leading through to a dining room. Alicia lit it up.

They carried on through the house, Alicia lighting the way,

until every lamp on the lower floor was burning. The air was cool, and Brent had gotten a little used to the scent. Sure enough there was damp laundry in a plastic hamper in the laundry.

Nathan Brooks had had good appliances. A new Westinghouse washer and drier set stood against the laundry's wall, as if never actually used.

At the bottom of the stairs, Alicia stopped. Stared up.

"He was up there," she said. "When they found him. On his bed."

Somewhere she had mentioned that she would be claiming the body tomorrow. A local funeral home would take care of all the details.

"Encourage me," Alicia said.

"Do you want for me to go up first?"

"Not like that."

Then he was tongue-tied. What did she mean, 'encourage me'. This was definitely outside of his skillset.

What would he say to a new trainee when they headed over to Fairbanks for a live exercise with a training aircraft fuselage blaze.

Check your gear. Check the hose. No heroics. Your own safety is paramount.

Didn't make much difference, really. Someone would either dive into a conflagration to rescue a child, or they would freeze. No amount of training could get around how someone might feel in the moment.

So how did Alicia feel in this moment?

He put his right hand on the small of her back. It was

meant to be reassuring, but he realized it could be taken easily as in invasion of personal space. You didn't touch someone else without their permission.

But her left hand came around and fumbled a moment before taking his.

He hadn't misread it at all.

Though if he was about to go hand in hand up a set of stairs with an alluring woman, he would have hoped for better circumstances.

And there he went, thinking about this sexually, rather than as just a plain human connection. A necessary connection.

Alicia would have taken anyone's hand. Calie's. Red's. Even taken Cheyenne from the diner's hand. Alicia just needed someone with her as she went up those stairs.

As they went up, together, step by step, Brent remembered his own parents. How would it be for him in his own father's house, going up the stairs to the room where he'd died?

Patrick Naylor was still very much alive and continuing to ply his trade as a doctor in Spokane. The man was in good health and would probably never retire. He would still be doctoring into his nineties, even as Brent himself would be wondering about whether to stay in Alaska or head down to Florida with all the other retirees.

Or maybe somewhere not quite so muggy. Maybe Oklahoma.

He shook his head at himself as he and Alicia reached the stairway landing. Halfway up.

"What?" she said, noticing his fractional head shake.

"Just wondering what you might be going through," he said. "I can't imagine this. You were so far removed from him and–"

She put her right index finger on his lips.

"Hush now," she said.

Talking too much. Of course, his initial instincts to keep quiet were the right ones.

They continued on up.

One of the steps squeaked loudly under his weight, and he slowed a moment.

Alicia looked back at him.

"I'd imagined a fixer-upper," she said. "But that's the first thing I've seen that needs work."

Brent just nodded.

The top floor hallway wasn't carpeted, but there was a long dark rug laid out over the polished pine floors. Framed photographs hung on the walls. Black and white, and color. People. Places.

Kids playing on a bright plastic playground under brilliant summery skies, with trees in the background.

Alicia went up to the photograph.

"Me," she said. "And David. This might have been down in Paris." She glanced at Brent. "Paris, Texas."

Brent smiled. "They have their own Eiffel Tower, don't they?"

She smiled back. "Yeah. With a cowboy hat."

She moved along to the next photo. Her and David, but older. In an aluminum dinghy at the edge of a lake. Then, a photo of just David, holding a hammer over a piece of roof framing. Then David again, astride a motorcycle, leaning back with his arms folded, wearing aviator sunglasses and a loose sea-captain's hat.

"Brando," Brent said, then remembered he was trying to keep quiet.

"He would have been about seventeen? Imagining himself the coolest thing since the discovery of Alaska."

Brent smiled. "I see what you did there."

Alicia smiled at him again. Warm, friendly. This was good. Seeing how her father was celebrating his family.

She stopped at the first door. There were five along the hallway. Probably three bedrooms and a bathroom? The one at the far end looked like it was just another cupboard. Perhaps access to the ceiling.

Alicia drew a deep breath.

"The moment," she said. "Moment of truth. Though, honestly, I don't know which of these bedrooms was his. Nor which one he was found in."

The neighbors had dropped around for a quiet visit, apparently, as they often did. When he didn't respond, they'd gone around the house, calling for him, finally finding him sprawled on a bed, mouth hanging open, already cold.

The first room had a double bed with a plump, hand-stitched red and maroon quilt, mixed in with occasional swatches of a few other colors. It looked warm and comfortable.

An old wooden desk stood against the wall, near the window with a positively ancient wooden desk chair—no wheels, just four legs spreading from a threaded steel support. From the days before those air-piston adjustment things. More like a piano stool.

Alicia wandered the room. She opened the free-standing closet and looked over the books in the bookcase next to it. Rifled through the papers on the desk.

She sat herself in the chair.

Brent stayed by the door. The air was thicker and warmer upstairs. Expected. The scent was more pleasant. Clean, as if the furniture had been polished with pine fragrance.

"He would have sat here," she said. "Writing letters. Letting the congresswoman know what a screw up she was making of her attempts at policy. Letting the governor have an earful. Making sure that David and I knew that he was all right and doing fine and reminding us that we could come visit any time, but understood that we had busy lives."

Brent just nodded.

Alicia tapped a pen on the desk.

"I kind of wish that he hadn't gone before he could have had grandkids." She looked around at Brent. "He was barely sixty."

"You want kids?" Brent said.

"Of course." She swallowed and looked out the window. "But that ship may well have sailed, as they say."

Outside the darkness was growing. A flickering of street-lights shone through, but her wan reflection showed in the glass.

"There's tons of time," Brent said, immediately worried

that he was saying the wrong thing. "You're what, twenty-eight." Then he worried that he had gone too high.

She laughed. "I'm thirty-six."

"Oh," he said.

"You're very flattering," she said.

"I'm lousy with ages. I actually wondered if I might have offended you by saying twenty-eight. You know, too old."

She actually laughed. "Quite the charmer, huh?"

In that moment he was suddenly much more attracted to her. So sweet and cute and cutting.

And yet it was an utterly inappropriate location to even mention that.

Not that he would really know how.

He just stood there, like a big lug, half-smiling. Hoping that he was helping her out at least.

That's all he should be thinking about, really.

He kind of had to blank his mind. Blank out anything else.

It wasn't easy, though. She was just so nice.

Chapter Thirteen

Alicia sat at her father's desk.

The hard wooden top was worn and pitted from years of her father working on it. Or other people? Perhaps he'd just bought it secondhand when he'd arrived in Candleton.

There were pages of notes lying on the desk. Yellow legal pads, and plain white copy paper and school exercise books. As if he was trying to put things in order, but couldn't quite get it together.

She lifted one of the pads and read a few lines. Fishing ties and gardening advice. A little bit about himself. A time when he'd gotten tangled in a roots at the edge of a river and fallen in.

Stories of his life.

Had he been writing a book about himself? These were more like notes for a project than a diary.

She rifled through the pages. Hundreds of them. Notes in pencil and ballpoint. Black and blue. Some sketches. Birds and baseball caps and tree-covered slopes.

He might have even been a fair artist.

She looked up and out through the window. Out across the steep roofs of Candleton. Dark and brooding trees. Streetlights and power lines. Off in the distance stood the dark silhouette of a church tower, and far beyond that lay mountains. There were mountains everywhere in Alaska. The opposite of most of Oklahoma.

Alicia ran her hands across the desk's top. The wood was warm and the surface contour was reassuring. As if there was a part of him left in it.

She was conscious of Brent still standing back at the door-way. Watching. Silently.

What was going on with her? Why had she dragged him up here? Why was she wanting him to stay now. Was it the comfort of anonymity? She didn't know him, so she didn't have to behave a particular way.

He was being quite remarkable really. Just accepting. Just being quiet and letting her process this the way she needed to.

Perhaps that was just the Alaskan way. A strong, silent type. Perhaps that was all she was attracted to. Perhaps any other local man would be arousing those same feelings in her.

She glanced back at him. He was just standing there, an odd smile on his face.

"All right?" he said, but quietly. He wasn't pushing anything. Wasn't making her go faster than she needed to.

But nor was he running off and abandoning her to it.

A good man.

Calie had said as much.

But then Calie had practically been playing matchmaker, and now was not the time.

Alicia drummed her fingers on the desk.

"Yes," she said. "I'm all right. At least, as all right as I might be."

He'd tried to guess her age. And had been a real gentleman about it. With some guys, that might have been cheesy or even kind of creepy.

But on him, it was sweet.

If only she could stop thinking about him and focus on what she needed to do here.

Get through her father's estate.

She leaned back and looked around at Brent.

"Twenty-eight, huh?" she said.

Chapter Fourteen

Brent stayed against the door frame in silence. From the road outside came the quiet rumble and hiss of a passing pickup.

Alicia sat at her father's desk. Leaning back in the old wooden office chair.

"Twenty-eight, huh?" she said.

"I'm just not very good with ages," he said. "Calie will tell you. I undershot her by a few years."

"I bet you did." Alicia got to her feet. "Let's see the rest of the house. Three rooms to go."

She sped by him with a little sudden burst of energy. Brent followed her through.

Beyond the master bedroom lay the bathroom, with a big tub with a shower rose high on the wall, and a curtain enclosing the tub.

Across the hall was a junk room, with another desk,

stacked high with papers and books and broken electronic equipment, with more boxes on the floor, some stacked beyond waist high.

"Oh, boy," Alicia said. "This is David's territory."

"Your brother?"

"He would just get a Dumpster and toss everything in. Me, I feel as if I need to go through it."

"Really?"

"Well, you know. What if there's an old photo album of my great-grandmother's wedding?"

"Or the deed to a mine."

"Exactly! You know what I mean."

"I guess. You just do it one box at a time. Haul it downstairs and tip it out and go through it."

"With the fire lit and a glass of wine?"

"And Coldplay on the stereo, turned down low."

She laughed, turning to him. Her hand came up and landed on his sternum, right at his collarbone. The hand lingered a moment.

"You know me too well," she said, dropping her hand.

"You think?"

A smile. "Nope. The obvious stuff. But really you've just begun to scratch the surface."

"Begun?"

"Well, we can still talk some more. Tonight. I'm still hoping that you'll stay." She stepped around him and went to the next bedroom.

It was made up as a guest room, with a single bed draped with another handmade patchwork quilt. On a bedside table stood a clock, a photograph of Alicia, David and their father. It looked like the Grand Canyon in the background.

There were two books there. Alicia stepped over and picked them up.

"*Goosebumps*," she said. "*Night Of The Living Dummy*. And this one is *Ella At Farnsworth*. My favorite, when I was a kid."

"*Goosebumps?*"

She held it up. "That's David. It's like he's left the room ready for us to..." She took breath. "For us to come visit."

She dropped the books on the quilt and fled the room. Brent heard her solid footfalls on the stairs. As if she was going down two at a time.

Hope she's holding the railing, the search and rescue part of him said.

A couple minutes later, Brent found her in the kitchen. She'd drawn a glass of water and was staring out into the back yard. There was a big pine there, and a garden shed. The ground looked scrubby and wet.

"Sorry," she said, without turning around.

"Nothing to be sorry for." He came up and stopped about a foot back from her.

The kitchen light flickered. Perhaps the utilities were going to be shut off soon. So many little things to work out when you were trying to take care of an estate.

"When I was little," Alicia said. "I mean, really little, he would read to us in the evenings. Gritty stuff. *The Lord of The Rings*, *The Lord of The Flies*. And the really old stuff. Mark Twain and Charles Dickens. David is three years older than me, so perhaps it was to keep his interest, I suppose."

Out in the yard, a golden striped cat stalked along by the back fence, eyes glowing in the dim light.

"When David got older, and was reading to himself, it was the horror stuff. The *Goosebumps* and whatever. Pretty soon it was the early Stephen King and Dean Koontz books. Mom said that David just *devoured* them. Books the size of a brick."

"Not your thing, huh?"

Alicia shuddered. "I can barely look out into the yard here without imagining some shadowy guy standing in the back corner watching me."

She turned.

"Creepy old house," she whispered.

"Pretty well lit," Brent said, unsure what to say that would make it all right. It felt like a little bit of a tightrope, really. The house where her father had died.

Brent wished he had the answers. Wished he could find the right thing to say.

"Still," he said. "You're not staying anyway. You'll get it tidied up and get all the official forms and such signed off, then you'll–"

Again her finger was on his lips. She'd stepped right up to him.

Close. He could smell her wonderful deep scent. Womanly. Musky. Desirable.

Brent had to take a breath himself. When had he felt so attracted to someone. He didn't even know her. Not really.

But there was something he knew, right now. That there was a connection between them. Intangible, but real.

Her finger was still on his lips.

He put his hand on her elbow. Slipped his other hand around her back.

Alicia's finger dropped. Her hand stopped, resting on his pec.

A charge ran through him. As if that physical touch had brought tangibility to their connection.

"Alicia," he whispered.

She stared into his eyes, her pupils so wide it was as if he could fall right in.

"The man who pulled me from the burning wreck of an airliner."

She winked.

Wow. She was just so disarming.

"You walked off the airliner," he said, with a smile. "The fire never even started. And it's not a wreck. They'll have it fixed by the end of the day and it will be flying back to Juneau tomorrow."

His eyes flicked out the window again. It was already the end of the day.

Much too late to even consider driving back to Wilkes Landing.

"I'll have to stay over," he whispered.

"Yes you will," she said, her voice husky.

Brent felt a surge and he bent forward to kiss her.

She turned her face up to his.

Their lips brushed, but almost right away, Alicia stepped back.

"Sorry," Brent said. It had felt like a moment. Clearly, yet another moment that he had misread.

"No, I'm sorry," Alicia said. "I just..."

"It feels wrong. In the house where your father died."

She shivered and right away he felt awkward. Should never have voiced that.

"Exactly right," she said. "I know it sounds very clichéd, but you're absolutely right." Her eyes flicked toward the ceiling.

Brent stepped back, but she stepped with him. Her hand came up to his chest again.

He put his arms around her. There was nothing sexual to it at all. Just two people. One offering comfort, the other accepting it.

But, boy did she feel good in his arms. He had to push those kinds of thoughts aside. There was a time and a place. He didn't know where that was, but sure as eggs, it wasn't here.

"I'm a strong woman," she said.

"I could tell."

"So why am I feeling so hollow and cut up?" She was leaning into him now. Her arms slipped around his back. She tilted her head in against his shoulder.

"Anyone would," Brent said. "I would."

"Differently, though. Stoic and organized, I'm sure."

"We never know how we'll react to grief. It's a complicated emotion."

"How come you're so wise?"

"Me? More like I'm making it up as I go along."

"Well it's working. Keep holding me a moment."

"As long as you need." Nah, that sounded wrong too. So he

shut up. Just kept his arms around her. She felt warm and snug in his grasp.

Outside, the cat had apparently crossed the yard and was now sitting on the wall right outside the kitchen windows, right above the sink bench.

The cat watched Brent with narrowed eyes. Suspicious.

I have good intentions, Cat, Brent said silently.

It felt like fifteen minutes, but was probably only a couple, when Alicia stiffened a little and adjusted her pose.

Brent let go.

"I suppose you do need to go huh?" she said.

"Well, I do have a rostered day off tomorrow, though there's probably paperwork on todays incident to take care of."

"I bet."

"Though Calie and Red can probably manage both of those. They'll call me, I guess, if they need anything."

And they shouldn't. One thing that the airport was pretty good at was avoiding interrupting days off, save for a genuine emergency. They knew, as did Brent, that time away to refresh and reset were as important at time on the job. They needed him and the others functioning at their best.

"All right," Alicia said. "So, would you like to stay? I can sleep down here on the sofa and you can take the spare room upstairs."

"I will." He smiled at her. "I guess we should eat. Properly. Something more nutritious than cookies." Brent cast his eyes around the kitchen. "I might even be able to whip something up from ingredients that he has here."

The cat had stood up on its hind legs and was scratching at the window.

"Maybe we need to feed the tawny lion out there too."

Alicia turned.

"Drumlin?" she said. "Really."

The cat dropped down and yawned.

"You know the cat?"

"She was a just a kitten the last time I saw Dad. She's grown into a monster." Already Alicia was heading around to the back door.

Chapter Fifteen

B rent followed Alicia through a small mudroom and the unlocked back door. There was a another veranda, much smaller than out front.

Alicia had stepped off the back steps and onto the muddy ground.

"Drumlin?" she called. "Drumlin. Puss, puss. Come on. Drumlin. Come on puss."

The cat had leaped from the outside kitchen windowsill and now strolled across toward where Alicia had crouched.

But the cat stopped. It lowered its ears and sniffed at her. Its tail dropped.

"Drumlin," Alicia said. "Come on sweetie." Alicia made an odd kind of kissing sound with her lips.

The cat's tail went up and curled back and forth.

"There you go, Drumlin." Alicia made the kissing sound again and the cat strode forward.

Alicia put out a hand and Drumlin stretched forward to sniff at it. Then Drumlin ducked her head under Alicia's hand and pushed up.

"There you are," Alicia said. "Sweetie." She scratched Drumlin's chin and ears as Drumlin twisted and turned to bring the right part of her head to bear.

"Purring," Alicia said.

"What's she been doing?" Brent said. "Has someone been feeding her."

Alicia looked around at him. "Drumlin has always been pretty self-sufficient. At least that's what I heard in my infrequent communications with Dad. She could disappear for a few days at a stretch and show up looking fatter than ever."

"Local friends, or squirrels and jays?"

"I'm sure she has another family around, don't you sweet-ie." Alicia's voice changed into pet-talk over the last three years, and she scooped Drumlin up into her arms. Alicia stood, cuddling and rubbing her chin against the top of Drumlin's head. Again, Drumlin pushed back.

Brent reached up and scratched Drumlin's jawline.

"Cute," Brent said. "Independent. A survivor."

"She is. Runs in the family." Alicia met his eyes again. Outside in the dim light, she looked quite stunning.

"I can tell," Brent said. "So, should we feed her?"

"You bet. There's probably kibble and canned meat at least."

Drumlin's eyes were closed and she was leaning into Alicia.

Back inside, Alicia set Drumlin down, and Drumlin proceeded to make figure eights around Alicia's calves.

Brent opened the pantry and found a bag of Science Diet kibble. Open, but sealed up with clothes pegs.

"Bowl," Alicia said, pointing to a spot in front of the oven.

"Got it." Brent poured into the little silvery bowl. The kibble tinkled in and Drumlin came over and stood, staring at it.

"What?" Brent said.

Drumlin sat back on her haunches and looked up at Brent.

"Stir it," Alicia said.

"Stir it?"

"With your finger."

"Stir it with my finger?"

"Is that just too complex of a set of instructions there?" Alicia grinned at him.

"Not at all." Brent crouched and put his finger into the kibble. He stirred it up.

Drumlin made a cute little *chirrup* sound and pushed his hand out of the way with her head. She started eating.

"Cats, huh?" Brent said, standing.

"No worse than people."

"You think?"

"I've been dealing with people for quite some time now. Let me tell you, that cats are far more straightforward."

"I can't disagree." Brent leaned back against the sink bench. "Hungry?"

"Not really."

"All right then."

"All I've had today was whatever we had for breakfast at house, and then a couple sandwiches at the airport, then those two half cookies."

"Sounds like a wrestler's diet to me."

"Silly. But really, I should eat. In fact you should tell me that. To keep my strength up."

"You should eat," he said. "To keep your strength up. I saw some dry pasta in the pantry, and jars of pasta sauce. I could whip something up, I bet."

"You could?"

"Pasta and sauce, what could I possibly do wrong?"

"My last boyfriend could. He'd boil the pasta dry and wouldn't even realize until the fire alarm went off. And even not then, because he would think that the alarm was just one of the sound effects in whatever dumb blow-everything-up video game he was playing."

"Gamer," Brent said. "Who burns pasta."

"I can pick 'em, that's for sure." She counted off on her fingers, the way that Cheyenne had back at the little café. "The football fiend, the motorcycle fiend, the gaming fiend–whom I already mentioned–the lady's man, the Mommy's boy, the second football fiend, the wannabe movie-director, the lawyer and the buys-too-many-flowers-and-chocolates fiend."

"Quite the list. The lawyer sounds like a keeper."

Brent opened the pantry again and took out the bag of pasta–seashells–and the jar of sauce.

"Do you, my friend," Alicia said, "know how many hours a lawyer works when they're trying to make partner in ten years."

"One hundred and sixty-eight hours a week, I'm guessing."

Alicia grinned. "Spot on. It's also cute that you know how many hours there are in a week."

Alicia opened up the fridge. "Look. Grated cheese." She pulled out the bag.

"Perfect."

So then they were cooking together. There were no fresh vegetables, but Alicia got a frozen bag of mixed greens. They boiled up the pasta and vegetables separately and added in the sauce. The smell was heavenly.

"Does it count as home-cooked," Brent said, "if it all came out of packages?"

"If you cook together, it does."

"Already we're becoming domestic."

Alicia blinked at him and smiled.

"Sounds nice, I suppose. I come to Alaska to bury my father and hook up with an aviation fire-fighter."

Brent stirred the pasta pot, getting the pasta mixed through well with the tomatoes and onion and basil.

Was she saying the things that he couldn't? Voicing it?

Hook up with an aviation fire-fighter.

All the while knowing the impossibility of any 'hook up'. It wouldn't go anywhere. Couldn't last.

Or could it?

"I'll be right back," she said, and slipped off through the mud room and the back door.

Brent watched her go into the yard.

He felt for her. Dealing with the death of her father.

Dealing with Brent being a little too casual and off-hand. Maybe he should go after dinner.

It wasn't like the road would be so very bad anyway.

Alicia stood out in the yard, and stepped off toward the side. She got her phone from a pocket and shone the light around.

Brent kept stirring. A good hearty dinner, then perhaps on his way off home. It had been good being in her company for a few hours. Longer.

Actually, better than good. It had been great. She had a nice energy and intelligence.

All of that a little tempered by the loss of her father.

Wouldn't it have been great to have had the opportunity to have gotten to know her better without that hanging over them. Over her.

Ah, well. Circumstances didn't always play out.

"Hey," Alicia said, right in the kitchen, startling him. He'd been off in dreamworld and hadn't even realized she'd come back in.

"Hey," he said.

"Cilantro." She held up a green sprig of the herb. "I don't know how Dad got it to grow up here, but it'll be great in the pasta, don't you think?"

"I do," Brent said with a smile.

Alicia touched his arm and set the sprig down on the bench.

She leaned in close. She smelled a little of the night air now. Of the garden.

"You're doing great," she said. "I'm really glad you're here."

"Thanks. Me too. Now, got take a seat and let me chop this cilantro and finish up the meal."

"A seat?"

"At the dining table. Take a weight off for a moment. Maybe there's some wine or some beer somewhere?"

"This is my father we're talking about. If there was none, then I'd think we'd come to the wrong place."

"Oh."

"No, it's fine. He was a drinker, I suppose, but not a drunk. I hope. I think he was more of a connoisseur? Fine wines and imported beers. Triple distilled, double malt fine Irish whisky or whatever they do to it over there."

"How about that?" He didn't know much about fancy liquor.

"Where would he keep the good stuff, though?" Alicia said. "That's the question."

"Why don't you go find it, and I'll finish up here. I'll holler when dinner's ready."

"You bet." Alicia leaned in close and kissed him on the cheek.

Brent stood there stunned a moment as she went out through the mudroom. Then he smiled and got on with chopping the cilantro to stir through the pasta.

Chapter Sixteen

A licia found herself laughing through dinner. Brent had some tales of some of the people he'd helped out over the years. People who should have known better.

The guy who'd felled a tree onto his cabin, without damaging the house too much, but then he'd hitched up a tractor to the tree to haul it off.

"The tractor lurched forward," Brent said, tapping his fork into his plate of pasta. "The tree jerked with it. But he had the chains tied all wrong. The tree fell through the cabin's roof, and the tractor ran into a hole, tipped over and he got trapped underneath."

"And you got him out."

"I helped, sure. But if he'd just gotten his chainsaw and cut away some of the tree, it would have worked out fine."

"I suppose if he'd cut the tree so it fell on his cabin in the first place, he wasn't thinking things through so well."

"I guess not."

The pasta was just marvelous. Which was kind of amazing really, since it was just out of the cupboard, save for the cilantro.

"You must have stories too," Brent said. "Developers must try on a few things."

"Oh boy. They really do. And then they honestly get surprised when they discover that they're not allowed to put up a block of sixteen homes, with no garages or parking. Or that there are load limits to flooring and walls."

"Cutting corners."

"Always."

They talked over the pasta, and over a nice Sauvignon Blanc white wine she had found amongst some others in a cupboard in the upstairs junk room. There seemed to be little other liquor around, which was kind of reassuring, really. Her father hadn't been up here drinking his life away.

Soon, though, despite the great company, she found herself yawning. Her back was a little achy too.

They cleaned up and checked in the living room for sleeping arrangements for Brent. Somewhere along the way, he'd insisted that she shouldn't have to take the sofa. She should have the spare bed.

It was clear that neither of them would sleep in her father's bed.

Alicia had hoped for a fold out sofa-bed in the living

room, but both sofas were dedicated, single-purpose only, with cushions that were stitched in. They couldn't even pull them off to lay on the floor in a row.

"It's fine," Brent said. "I can bend my knees, or stretch my feet up over the armrest."

They found sheets and blankets and created the makeshift bed, among some giggling and silliness. It was good having him around.

So good.

She shuddered imagining if she had been here alone. That would have been all right, in its own way, but having him was buoying her when she might have become too maudlin.

He showered upstairs and brushed his teeth with tooth-paste on his finger. He showered and came out of the bath-room, draped in a towel.

"Really?" he said, looking at the pajamas she was holding up for him. They were dark blue with little stylized cartoon images of palm trees and parrots forming a regular pattern.

"I guess you're about my father's size," she said.

"I can't wear your father's pajamas."

"And I can't have a naked hunk of a man in my father's house."

"Oh." He was holding the towel with one hand about his waist.

His hairy chest was still damp and she was able to have a second opportunity in the space of little more than a day to try not to ogle him.

"Hunk, huh?" he said, reaching to take the pajamas.

"Don't get full of yourself over it."

"Well, you're not so bad yourself."

They stood there in the upstairs hallway, just outside the bathroom door, with steamy vapor still spilling out, just a couple of feet apart.

"You think I'm a hunk?" she said.

"In a kind of feminine way."

She giggled. "You have an odd way with compliments."

"Oh I could go on all night."

"I'm sure. Put on the pajamas. Get downstairs. I need a shower too. I'll see you in the morning."

Somehow, as she stepped by, she managed to keep her hands off him. She closed the bathroom door and leaned back against it.

Too many emotions running through her right now. Far too many.

She got the shower going and had the vain hope that perhaps it would help wash some of them away.

The hiss of the water was invigorating, though, and the swirl of steam took her to another world.

It didn't matter about all the emotional stuff. Not for the moment.

Not under the wonderful pounding heat of the water of her back.

She was here. She'd made it.

Still in one piece. Almost.

Now she just had to get very organized about it. Treat it like a development contract. Work through the details.

One after the other.

Practical and efficient.

It would only be a little harder with a hunk of a man in the house while she tried to concentrate.

Chapter Seventeen

In the deep darkness, Alicia lay in the soft bed in her father's spare room.

She should be able to sleep. The bed was so comfortable and the quilt was so warm. Warm and heavy. It was like being a child again. Feeling safe and looked after.

Except that just across the hallway, her father had died.

Tomorrow would be better. She knew that sleep would come. Eventually.

In the morning, Brent would go, no matter how much she wished that he would stay. It would be for the best.

She could work on sorting out the house.

Maybe she should have found a motel in town and stayed there. Just to give herself some space from the house. It was kind of too close.

With her thoughts continuing to swirl, she did sleep, and

found herself waking with strong light blading through the slit in the room's curtains, and some kind of banging downstairs.

At first she thought it was Brent. Perhaps making breakfast. Perhaps using a hammer to fix that squeaky board in the stairs.

She got up and pulled one her light robe. It was her favorite, a dark red with stitched images of Japanese cranes wading in water. Too thin, though, in the cool air. She'd traveled light, with just the carry-on, but really she should have brought a checked bag.

She might be here longer than she'd expected or anticipated.

From downstairs, she heard voices.

Men's voices.

One of them sounded a little consternated. Alicia took a breath. Who used that word?

Annoyed?

That was a better word.

Wearing her robe over her own pajamas–a baggy tee shirt with matching brushed cotton ankle-length pants–she hurried down. The squeaky stair squeaked as she stepped on it.

The front door was wide open and Brent was there, in the tropical-themed pajamas, just closing it.

"What's going on?" Alicia said, as she came down the last few steps.

"I guess I met your brother."

"David? He's here?"

Brent pointed to the living room.

Alicia came off the stairs and went through the door.

David was standing there, facing her, but looking at the sheets and blankets and pillow draped across the sofa.

David was wearing tan chinos and a black button shirt. Pressed. He had black loafers on his feet and a pair of black Blues Brothers sunglasses in his hand, hanging by one of the arms.

Same old always, really. A certain image to maintain.

Alicia had a dozen or a hundred questions for him, but instead she turned to Brent.

"Did you sleep alright there?" she said.

"I slept like a rock," he said. "Herd of buffalo couldn't have woken me. You?"

"I wouldn't have noticed any buffalo. Much too caught up in my own thoughts."

"You should come get a job in Search and Rescue. It wears you out so that you never have time for anxiety or indecision."

"Or a social life?"

"Well, there is that."

"Hello?" David said. "Sibling here, while the two of you are jabbering. Remember me?"

"Vaguely," Alicia said. "David, you said? Sounds like you might have had some very conservative parents there."

"You're telling me." David grinned. "Come here."

Alicia went over as he stepped to her and he wrapped her up in a tremendous hug.

It felt so good to be close to him even if for just a moment. He smelled of airplane and children and home. A David smell.

So long since she'd inhaled that scent and it carried her right back to grade school and family picnics.

He kept holding on, and she kept right on holding on back.

They'd lost their father. He'd gone, orphaning them.

David felt both strong and frail at once. Both the family comfort she needed, and the gangly, goofy kid he'd been, needing his sister's level-headedness to get him through something. Usually getting ditched.

"Hey," he said, and let go, jarring her.

"I'm glad you're here," she said. "How did you get here? When? Why didn't you let me know?"

David smiled. "Hey, that's my sister all right. Always with the questions. Dot, dot, dot." He jabbed his finger as if stabbing at the button for an elevator or a crosswalk. "Always one after another."

"Well," she said. "Last I heard you were too busy to be bothered."

"That's not fair. I have a life. He chose to come up here and turn into a hermit." David glanced at Brent. "No offense."

Brent just smiled. He was hard to read. David doubtless thought that Brent should say something like 'none taken', but he hadn't. The comment wasn't directed at him.

Besides, Alicia was kind of mad with David. Firstly for not showing any interest, and secondly for showing up out of the blue like this.

"I got your texts," David said, holding up his phone. He read from the display. 'I will come back to your place with a dump truck filled with Dad's stuff and just leave it on your lawn'. Nice."

"You must have already been on your way," Alicia said.

"I was."

"I could make coffee," Brent said. "Once I'm dressed." He came through the room and gathered up the neatly folded stack of his clothes. He turned and went back through to the hallway.

"Good to meet you," he said. "I'm glad you're here."

Then Brent was gone, presumably to dress in the privacy of the bathroom. Alicia heard his footfalls on the stairs.

A tinge of guilt washed over her, since he'd just been driving her up, and now he'd stayed, without a change of clothes. Without even a toothbrush.

"So who is this guy?" David said. "Your boyfriend? I thought you were single."

"Because you do such a good job of staying in touch and keeping track of whom I'm dating."

"Back at you sis." David pushed the sheets and blankets aside and plonked himself down on the sofa. "Looks like a keeper, but you make him sleep down here on the sofa. What, did you two have a fight?"

He'd been in the house all of three minutes and already he was being infuriating. He should have just stayed in Tishomingo or Paul's Valley or whichever little town he was living in now.

A fine one he was to talk about hermits. He'd gone off and isolated himself out in rural Oklahoma. Doubtless he would say he was within twenty minutes of the freeway, which put him within just another hour or so of OKC. From there, it was only another hour and a half on the Turnpike to reach her.

Back at you sis.

How much effort had she really made? Wasn't she just a little caught up with her friends and her life in Tulsa. Racquetball on a Thursday and drinks on a Friday and hikes out through the wonderful forests around Lake Absolom on a Sunday morning.

But then, every time she had ever tried to contact him, he really just rebuffed her. Monosyllabic answers on phone calls, and texts to which he never replied. Leaving her on 'seen' on Messenger.

"You pushed me away," she said, feeling a little heat of anger rising. "You left the city for the wilderness, which was fine. You live your life now however you want. But don't suddenly show up here when I'm trying to deal with Dad's death."

"You're trying to deal with Dad's death? Where were you when he got sick the first time? Huh? What were you doing? Flying off around the country trying to sell substandard housing to people who can't afford it anyway. Tearing up the land for new developments that are just simple money-printing rorts."

"That's not fair. You know nothing about what I do." Her volume was rising. How could this idiot be her brother? How could it be that every time they saw each other they just bickered. They should be adults.

Wait. There was something else he said.

Dad had gotten sick earlier?

"Of course I don't know," David said. "But I can figure it out. I looked into your company. You know that? Filled in swamps and bulldozed habitats. You're just—"

"Wait," she said. "Dad got sick?"

"You know about that. Eighteen months ago. More or less. He was in hospital overnight, but they sent him home again. His lungs."

"His lungs? I never knew. I thought he was doing fine up here. Whenever we spoke, that's what he said."

"Of course he would say that. His precious daughter shouldn't have to worry about him."

Alicia took a step back. David's words stung. All of it. About their father. About the company. About her.

This was exactly why they didn't communicate. They lived in different worlds. Had done for more than a decade.

Their father was all they had in common. And this house.

Beyond that, it was all just a big fat nothing.

But it should be enough.

"Tell me about him getting sick," she said. "Emphysema, I guess."

"Yes. Fluid. He had to be on oxygen. And blood tests. Nothing really showed up at all. Age, I guess."

"He was in his sixties."

"Maybe environment too. Who could stand this cold twelve months of the year?"

I could.

Alicia shivered. Where had that thought come from? Tulsa could get pretty cold, but nothing like this part of

Alaska. Frankly Tulsa would be considered tropical compared to even Juneau.

But not their father. What had been the attraction for him? The isolation, probably. David had perhaps wound up just like him, with that love of isolation.

And yet, Brent had a family. Right then, Alicia wanted to ask about Francine and the kids, Jake and Emily. And that immediately coupled with a shimmer of guilt. What kind of aunt was she being to those two.

Aged four and two.

She should see more of them.

After all, with the turnpike and the freeway, they were no more than a few hours away.

"How is Francine?" Alicia said. "And the kids?"

"Change of tack, huh?"

Alicia sat in the sofa opposite the one where Brent had slept.

"More like we don't need to bicker. Perhaps I'm getting the chance for a little self-reflection."

"You?"

"Ha, ha."

"No. I'm serious. You're the most self-absorbed person ever. Then you actually ask about Francine, and Jacques and Emily."

Jacques, huh. Even though David had always called the boy Jake.

Francine was French, so of course the children had French names.

"I'm trying here," Alicia said.

"Really. I've never known you to make any effort. Always taking the easy way out of things."

She stood again and headed out of the room. Had to, before she started yelling at him. What a jerk.

She went by the stairs, seeing Brent sitting there on the landing, just looking down.

Chapter Eighteen

B rent saw Alicia come to a stop at the bottom of the stairs. She looked up, startled. As if she'd forgotten he was in the house.

"Looking for a safe exit, huh?" she said. Her face was bleak. Sad. She was wearing a pretty bathroom robe that looked a little like a Japanese kimono. It suited her.

Right then he just wanted to hold her. All that she was going through, but adding in this was just making it harder for her.

"I guess I am," he said. "But I left my keys and wallet down there. And my phone." He managed a half a smile. "Figure I'm getting in the way now."

"You're not in the way. It's just family dynamics."

Which needed to play out the best way they could. Without some guy from another town sitting in.

Kind of a pity. He was enjoying her company.

And he really liked the house. The whole place was comfortable and homey. The kind of thing he'd never really been able to create back in Wilkes Landing.

Brent stood.

"Yeah," he said. "Family dynamics. And I'm not family, so I should butt out."

"You don't have to go."

"I really do. Sticking around just makes it harder for the both of you." Brent started down from the landing.

"Makes it easier for me," Alicia said.

Brent didn't know how to respond to that.

He reached the bottom of the stairs. Close enough to Alicia that he could see the flecks of icy white in her eyes. Her brows didn't seem severe now at all. Strong and full of expression.

She stared back at him.

"I'm glad," he said, managing to fumble out some words before he disappeared entirely into her. "Glad that I've made it easier. But now I'm intruding."

"You're not," she whispered, gorgeous lips barely moving. The words were barely about the sound of her breath.

"I doubt your brother would agree," Brent whispered back. "He was surprised to find me here. I get the definite sense that I'm an interloper."

"Nice word."

"Thank you."

"But he's the interloper."

"He's family." Brent glanced toward the living room. David

would be right there. If he couldn't make out the actual words, at least he would hear the breathy whispers.

"I know he's family," Alicia said. "But he just takes up so much space. In my head, I mean."

"I get that. And maybe it's not easy, but then again, maybe it will improve your dynamic."

"I doubt that."

"But there is less chance if I'm around. It would be as if I was on your side. And I would be. But then it's two against one, but I don't have any voting rights, so it would just make him annoyed and resentful."

Alicia gave him the slightest of nods.

"You're right," she said.

"I have to go."

Another slight nod. Her eyes were bleak and it tore at his heart right then.

How could it? After just a day.

Good grief, was he falling for her?

"I'll get my keys," he said. "And stuff. And get on my way."

He bent a little, to kiss her cheek, and she turned so that their lips brushed.

A charge ran through him. Had that been what he'd intended?

And their lips stayed brushing. Then pressed closer. She was so soft against him. Nerves fired off across his scalp and down his back and all over his body.

Her lips moved against his. Her tongue darted out, just touching his upper lip. His teeth.

His tongue.

Her breathing quickened. Deepened. His too.

Alicia's hands came up. Slid to his shoulder. Grabbed. Pulled him closer. Demanding. Eager.

He was too. Absolutely.

It was as if everything in the world fell away from him. The house. His job. Even where he was. His brain swirled into the kiss as it became everything there was anywhere.

She dropped her hands suddenly and pushed him back. They separated like a butterfly leaving a flower.

Brent smiled to himself. When had he become a poet? A *bad* poet at that.

"Well," he said, just staring her.

"Well," she said back.

"That... well that sure was—"

She put her finger on his lips again. It was at once both incredibly intimate, and quite disarming.

He nodded.

From the corner of his eye, he spied David, standing back in the living room.

The expression of his face was unreadable. Annoyance? Disgust? Anger?

Clearly he'd seen the kiss.

The kiss. Brent couldn't remember ever kissing anyone like that. Ever.

He had kissed a few people. Not many, and not one of them had brought such a sudden bolt like that. Like a kind of drug that was still coursing through his system.

"I'd best get on the road, then," some part of his other self said. As if there was an autopilot taking over an aircraft when the pilots had gone to sleep.

"Best, then," Alicia said, breaking their intense eye contact and looking over at David. "And you and I can spend the day fighting over how we deal with this." She waved her hand up, indicating the house.

"Alicia," David said. "Don't be like that."

"Don't be like..." she trailed off, leaving out the *what?*

She turned to Brent.

"You're welcome to stop by again," Alicia said, though it seemed her heart wasn't in it. "If you wanted. You know, in a few days. It looks like I'll be here for a while. I guess."

"You guess?" David said.

"Stay out of it. He's leaving. You can bicker all you like after."

David muttered, "Bickering's a two-way street." But he walked by them and vanished off along the hallway.

Alicia's shoulders sagged, as if the tension had drained away.

Brent felt melted to the spot. As if the soles of his shoes had gone tacky from a fire.

But he ripped himself from the floor and went into the living room to retrieve his keys and wallet and phone. He should have just left them in his jeans. Then he could have just marched on out the front door before any of this.

Except then there never would have been that kiss.

Partway across the living room floor, he stopped and turned. Drawn back to her.

But a cupboard door slammed in the kitchen, then came the sound of water running.

Enough to jar the moment. Enough to make him keep going.

Attractive as she was, and encouraged as he was, it was still a prickly moment.

He should just forget it and leave them to the business they clearly needed to do.

Though he would never forget this moment. Not ever.

Out on the veranda a cool gust blew through. The air in Candleton was warming as the sun crested the mountains.

Brent stopped right at the bottom of the steps. His pickup was still out on the street.

Alicia was right behind him.

"Well," she said, as he turned. "Thanks for all your help. You know, with a place to stay and driving me up here."

"No trouble."

Alicia had left the front door open and Brent could see David at the far end of the hallway. Heading for the front of the house.

"It was nice meeting you," Alicia said.

"Likewise." Had that burning intensity left her eyes? "I hope we can catch up again another time."

"I hope so too. Did we exchange numbers?"

Had they? There'd been no need. They'd essentially been together since after the airport incident. Brent slipped his wallet from his pocket and flicked through for one of his cards.

"They thought it was a good idea," he said, finding one and handing it to her. "Seems very old school."

She grinned, but didn't take the card.

"What?"

"Give me your phone," she said.

"Oh. Right." He took it from his back pocket and passed it to her.

"Unlock it," she said, passing it back.

"Yes of course." He tapped in his pin and handed over the phone again.

She tapped at the display for a moment and gave the phone back.

"Now you have my number," she said.

He looked at the display. *Alicia B*. She'd sent a text too.

Miss you.

He smiled up at her, wanting to kiss her all over again.

Maybe that would never pass.

Beyond, David reached the foot of the staircase and stopped. He was holding a glass of water.

"Yeah," Brent said to Alicia. "I miss you too."

She turned a little red, but smiled.

"Come on you two," David said. "Get it over with."

Alicia scowled, but didn't turn.

"I'll see you then," Brent said.

He saw the look in her eyes. There was too much coming at her. He couldn't have any expectations at all.

Despite the level of desire, it was practically impossible.

He wished it wasn't, but he had to be realistic about it.

"Will you?" she said. "See me?"

"Definitely." Spontaneously he reached and took her left hand with his right. Then put his other hand up too. She squeezed. Her skin was so soft, and her grip was so strong.

With him down a couple of steps, it was almost like he was on his knee, making a traditional proposal.

And from somewhere in all his churning thoughts, he'd said 'Definitely', which was like a commitment.

One thing that Brent Naylor did was honor his commitments.

"Definitely," he said, and turned, letting her hand slide from his, and he headed for his pickup.

Trembling.

He'd never felt so alive. So invigorated. So confused.

That all had to be a good thing.

He'd been getting in a rut, hadn't he? Or had he? His old life seemed so distant and unreal.

How had she done this to him?

He went around the hood and got in behind the wheel. Started up the truck.

Alicia was still on the veranda. Looking fantastic in her kimono robe.

She waved and Brent waved back. He pulled out into the street and headed for the route back to Wilkes Landing.

It felt as if it was going to be a long, lonely trip.

Chapter Nineteen

Alicia watched Brent's pickup's taillights shine red as he slowed for the intersection. Then he was around the corner and gone.

Out of her life.

Probably forever.

That kiss. She was still trembling from it. Her heart was still racing.

Right here in her father's house. Practically right under his bedroom.

"Come inside," David said from entryway. "It's cold with the door open."

Her brother. He'd been annoying since he'd been around. Back when they'd been growing up it had all just been sibling stuff. *She took my toy, he broke my phone, she hates my friends.* All of that.

But he should have grown out of it. *She* should have grown out of it.

Alicia went inside and closed the door.

"I'm taking a shower," she said, heading for the stairs.

"Are the utilities still on?"

A smart reply stalled on her tongue. Instead, she said, "Yes. I guess that's something we can look into today. Figuring out shutting those off. Working out if we sell the house, or rent it out, or what."

"I don't want a rental in Alaska. Can you imagine the problems?"

She held in another smart response. *Be the grown up.*

"I can," she said. "So let's scratch the rental. Look, I really need to clean up and get dressed. Did you have breakfast yet? There's food in the pantry."

He looked at her with narrowed eyes. "I didn't eat," he said. "My connection from Anchorage left really early."

"I could tell. Because here you are." She stepped forward and gave him another hug. "I'm glad you're here."

He hugged back. "Sorry if we got off on the wrong foot."

"That's just us, isn't it?"

He laughed. "I suppose so." He let her go and stepped back.

"I'll go take a shower," Alicia said. "Then we can get to it."

"Take your time."

The shower was fabulous. Hot and steamy, and the water pressure was great. Alicia soaped and rinsed, taking her time over it.

Imagining, for the briefest moment, sharing the shower with Brent.

She shut off the water and stood dripping behind the curtain for a moment. She needed to get a grip, that was for sure.

Soon she was dry and dressed. She checked her phone. There was the text from Brent's phone.

Miss you.

But she was the one who'd typed it in.

No more texts since.

"Of course," she whispered. "He's driving now."

With a couple of taps, she put his name into her contacts list, then headed back downstairs.

From below came the wonderful smell of spicy sweet oatmeal. David was cooking up a storm in the kitchen, and making a mess with it.

"Oh boy," Alicia said, casting her eyes across the spilled oats and sugar, and open canisters standing on the bench and the table.

David was at the stove, stirring a big pot. Drumlin stood on the sill outside, watching David with slitted, suspicious eyes.

"I make this for the kids," he said. "Old French recipe, though I had to improvise some of the ingredients. Dad has a well-stocked larder, but there's a lot of rice and a lot of cans of beets and asparagus."

"Not exactly breakfast foods." Alicia went through the mudroom and let Drumlin in. The cat chirruped at her and rubbed against her legs.

"Nope. So you've got chopped prunes, maple syrup, grated almonds, frozen blueberries, a few drops of vanilla essences, which frankly it surprised me to find, and lots of oats. *Lots* of oats."

"Sounds delicious."

"You look nice," he said, looking up and down in a brotherly kind of way.

"Thank you." She was just wearing jeans and black pumps and white DeCom exercise shirt. "I traveled light, but forgot that I should have brought a real winter coat."

"Just don't venture outdoors, you'll be fine. As long as the power holds out."

"Let's eat and then look over the bills and so on. Assuming that you're cooking for me too."

David looked into the pot as he stirred. "Looks as if I'm cooking for a family of ten. Improvising is not great. I kept adding oats since it looked too fruity."

"It smells great. What can I do?"

"Bowls, utensils. Maybe some brown sugar and milk." His face looked bleak then. "Milk. If there's milk it'll be well beyond its use-by date, right?"

"Probably." Alicia had opened the refrigerator the previous night and found the grated cheese, but she could not for the life of her remember anything else that had been in it.

The hinge squeaked as if it needed a little spray of WD-40.

Inside there were the remains of the bag of grated cheese, a whole bunch of things that ought to be thrown out—cucumber, lettuce, tomatoes—and some odd jars that looked like specimen bottles from a museum of unusual sea creatures.

She pulled one of the bottles out and read the label

"What is that?" David said.

"Artichokes. In brine."

"Oh, my favorite."

Alicia put the artichokes back and retrieved a carton of milk. The expiry date wasn't for another two days.

"He must have just bought it," she whispered. "The day he died."

"Gone bad?" David said.

"We've got a couple of days here." Alicia got the table set and they sat down to eat.

There was still some tension. She could feel it. Shrinks would have a great time here, looking at the two of them, identifying whatever they did and said as the responses to being here in their father's house.

The oatmeal, however, was delicious. Filling and hot and just what she needed.

"It's great," she said, as Drumlin pushed by her legs. Doubtless thinking that she deserved some breakfast too.

"Good, because it might be lunch too." David glanced at the pot.

She laughed and it felt good to actually do that.

"Sorry for being grouchy with you," she said.

"Sorry for being lousy at staying in touch."

"Likewise. Thanks for coming."

"Sorry for interrupting. If I'd realized that you were enter-taining someone I would have replied to the texts. Which I didn't get, I might add, until I stepped off the plane here in Candleton."

"Phone charge?"

"It was dead when I got to Anchorage, and I charged it but didn't turn it on. Then I remembered when I was on the plane up here. Little puddle-jumper of a thing. I think they had to unbolt the floats so they could land at the airfield instead of the lake."

"It's a different world, isn't it?"

"We think Oklahoma is provincial."

"We're positively cosmopolitan compared."

"There you go with the poetry. 'Positively cosmopolitan."

Alicia shrugged and took another mouthful. It really was good.

"I didn't mean to chase off your boyfriend."

"Yes you did, and he's not my boyfriend."

"Looked like it."

"Yeah." Now she was thinking about that kiss again. Wondering if she might ever get the chance to experience that again.

It would be fabulous to have had Brent still here, sharing their breakfast. There sure was enough of it.

But he was gone. Leaving her to deal with the estate and the city and her brother.

Which was how it should be. She couldn't let her naïve heart get in the way.

And yet it was.

Chapter Twenty

Alicia spooned up another mouthful of the delicious oatmeal. Just about enough to put all these things out of her mind. Brent. The city and their demands.

"Have you known him long?" David said from across the table. "A local?"

This was hard. She shouldn't have to be dealing with her father's death and feeling this kind of thing for a man. A man she'd only met yesterday.

Those same shrinks would probably tell her that it was entwined. Hooking up with some guy because of her emotional confusion following the loss.

Looking for a new male figure in her life.

"Alicia?" David said. "Your eyes are glazed."

"I know."

"Want to tell me about it?"

"You'll laugh."

"I won't."

"You can't know that. You'll think I'm silly and flighty and a mess."

"Maybe, but I also know that you're smart and quick and grounded, so it's a balance. Like most people, you're a complex mix of oats and maple syrup and dried fruit." He held his breakfast-laden spoon toward her.

"That's a terrible analogy."

"Make a better one."

"I am a swirl of peppermint in a chocolate fondue, with nuts and sherbet clusters draped over marshmallow."

He laughed. "We're as bad as each other."

"I know it. So, please don't laugh, but I met Brent yesterday. In Wilkes–"

"Yesterday!"

"Let me finish. Save all your judgement until the end."

David nodded and waved his spoon at her to continue, then put it in his mouth.

So she told him. The problem with the plane, the problems with the locals organizing somewhere for her to stay, the evening with Brent and Calie, and the drive up. Even the little stop at the café when she'd balked at the door.

David, to his credit, didn't laugh.

"Then," Alicia said, "I was too shaky, really, coming inside Dad's house, so I asked Brent to stay."

David nodded

"Go ahead," she said. "Judge away."

"Actually," David said, dipping his spoon into the last of his oatmeal, "the two of you spent more than a day together. More than a day and a half. Two nights. I've spun through entire relationships in less time. Remember Bex Antrim?"

"Could I forget?" A high school girl in David's year who'd had some kind of magic wand she could just cast at any boy who took her fancy. Love potion number nine or something.

"So I knew about her, right?" David said.

"Right..." Alicia smiled. It was good to be taken away from their father's house, away from thoughts of Brent.

"How she operated. But still, you know, teenage boys."

"I remember. I still have them ogling me, which is both flattering and disturbing."

"Yes. Apologies on behalf."

"Whatever. Tell your story."

"So one Friday I was walking home from the bus, and she'd gotten off the bus right after me. And she followed along about ten paces behind. The bus headed away and I'm walking along under all the street trees and over that rough old sidewalk and I get the tingling sense of someone behind me."

"Stalker."

"Exactly. Obvious now. So I stopped and turned. And she kept walking, right up to me. Until we were just about nose to nose."

"And she had a pretty nose."

"Oh my gosh. Like thin and with just the slightest of inward ski ramp curves."

"She was all curves."

"Yes she was. I never knew about peripheral vision until

that moment. I was staring into her eyes, but somehow taking her all in."

"Good grief. I don't need all of that. Just tell the story."

"So she said 'David', in this husky low voice. And I think I just about squeaked back 'Bex?', but with a real upward inflection. Then she's all like, 'I've seen you noticing me, but you've never done anything about it. Never asked me out'."

"Every boy noticed her, and the only ones game enough to ask her out were Brad and Travis."

"And Sebastien."

"Yep."

"I knew I was being played, but there was another part of my brain at work then so—"

"*Not* your brain."

"—I said 'Wanna go out?' and she said 'Sure, when? Tonight?' and I said 'Tonight's good.' and she said 'See you at seven'. Then she turned and walked away."

"Leaving you just a puddle on the sidewalk."

"Yep. An evaporating puddle. So we met up at seven, and got takeout and sodas and went down to Grail Pond and sat on the grass as the sun set. She talked about herself and her friends and how she was lonely and we made out some, which was spectacular. Then we were done and walking home and I said 'So can I see you tomorrow?', to which said something like 'In your dreams.' And that was that."

"You know," Alicia said. "You should get over that."

He laughed. "I am, believe me. I was just a kid."

"We all were. And you have Francine now. And Jacques and Emily. Family man."

"It's not all plain sailing."

"I bet. But at least you can sustain a relationship. Me, the sailing is rough and stormy and then the thing just sinks to the bottom."

"Sorry to hear that."

Alicia shrugged. She finished up her oatmeal and took the bowl to the sink. Drumlin came with her, rubbing whiskery cheeks against Alicia's calf.

"Thanks for breakfast," Alicia said, getting some kibble for Drumlin.

"Sure thing." David joined her at the sink, and suddenly she was aware of their size difference. He was just a half a head taller, but he had big shoulders and strong arms. She momentarily felt slight and fragile beside him.

He rinsed out his bowl and said, "So where do we start on all this?" He looked back through the kitchen. "It's pretty tidy."

"Refrigerator," she said. "And the pantry. We have to ditch any expired food."

"That's your priority?"

"It's a small thing and it will take a little bit of the weight off my mind."

"Good then."

"Oh." She remembered the city's plans. "Did you get the documents from the Candleton City Council?"

"Documents?"

"They want to tear down the house."

"They what?" Indignant. That was good.

"I have the papers upstairs. They were mailed to me."

"Snail-mail or email?"

"Email. But I printed them. I do that a lot. Habit I guess. Dealing with clients it's often easier to flick back through the pages. And then there are actual signatures in ink."

"No getting around those. Can I see the documents?"

"Of course. Give me a minute."

"I'll wash up."

"Thanks. I'll be right back down."

At the bottom of the stairs, Alicia checked her phone. Messages from her boss and another one from Olivia, but nothing from Brent.

Why was she expecting it?

She was being just like a teenager now. She puffed out her breath and headed upstairs to gather the documents to share with David.

Maybe they could actually fight it.

Chapter Twenty-One

Brent arrived back in Wilkes Landing hungry and tired and with a kind of a kink in his neck. That old sofa had definitely not been the best place to sleep. Not by a long shot.

He went straight to the airport. Slid the pickup in through the staff entry and parked near the grey of the fire house hangar. Alicia's little plane from yesterday's incident had been shifted along the tarmac, and was coned off. Fluttering strips of tiger-striped tape ran from cone tip to cone tip. A white, liveried pickup was parked in close and a woman in overalls stood on a three-step ladder looking into the engine, beneath the open cowling.

The inescapable stink of aviation fuel washed through the air.

The big green-yellow Oshkosh appliance was parked out

front of the fire house, looking shiny and glistening in the morning sun.

Across the far side of the tarmac, in front of the little row of commercial hangars, Judd Williams had his float plane out and was loading up some packages. A couple of hangars along, Ernie Williams, Judd's brother, was polishing the canopy glass on the *Williams and Fry* helicopter. They must have both got jobs on.

Even with everything swirling in Brent's head, and even with the emergency yesterday, life still went on in Wilkes Landing.

"Hey loverboy," Calie called from the Oshkosh's cab.

"That's getting real tired," he said. It almost stung. He'd felt so close to Alicia, but it had been so fleeting. As if she'd removed a piece of him and was holding it hostage in Candleton. That piece would be his heart and even he couldn't help but rolling his eyes at how kind of twee that sounded.

"You have a far away look in your eyes," Calie said. She'd dropped from the cab and was striding toward him.

"I do?"

"Omigosh!" Calie almost squealed. "She stole your heart! She did." Calie clasped her hands together. "That's so sweet. The two of you were just made for each other. I *knew* that sending you up there with her would be great. You got to spend some time with her." Calie danced around a little, shaking her hips and rocking her arms in and out, fists kind of pumping.

"Calie, please."

"So. When are you seeing her again?"

"No plans. How does–"

"No. Plans. Oh, boy, you have got to be kidding."

"Calie."

"Is she still there? Or wait, did she have a boyfriend waiting up there? Is that it? Is that why you look so glum? You give your heart away and next minute it's getting crushed by a runaway train loaded with steam rollers and stamping batteries."

"Calie. We have paperwork." Brent headed toward the fire house. The exterior needed a clean and the paint needed touching up in places. Maintenance on the building tended to get deferred when budgets came under the microscope.

"Paperwork," Calie said, "as the expression goes, schmaperwork."

Brent stopped. He looked at her, as she stared back at him with her guileless dark eyes. Her childlike enthusiasm was so often uplifting, but it could also, like now, become a little grating.

"Spill," she said, though a little more quietly.

"We got on great," he said. "We talked a lot. She has this delicious energy about her. But, Calie, she's dealing with her father's death. Having to clean up the estate. Then her brother arrived."

"Uh-oh. Brothers sure can get in the way."

"Yeah. They don't really get along, which made it even harder to stick around. They were the bicycle and I was the–"

"Third wheel! I know it. That's me all the time. Like last night. Getting in the way."

"You weren't in the way at all. It was good having you there."

"Aw!" Calie took three quick steps and wrapped him up in a firm hug. "You know," she said more quietly into his ear. "I have a good feeling about the two of you."

"You're sweet," Brent said, having to admit that it was actually comforting having Calie hugging him.

"I know it."

"But I have to be really practical. She's not staying in Alaska."

"So move to Iowa!"

"Oklahoma."

"See you've already started making plans."

"Just because I know where she lives, doesn't mean that I'm going to move there."

"I've been there." Calie let him go and stepped back. "You haven't. You'll love it."

Brent sighed. "Look, walk with me. You can bathe me in your wisdom as I get started on this paperwork." He glanced over at the parked plane with the engineer still under the cowling. "There are going to be reports from here to Anchorage."

"I saw them starting to come in. Response reports and 'learnings from the incident'. No injury lists and preparedness. We're going to be so busy with them, we'd better hope no more planes go down between now and Christmas next year."

"We hope that anyway. Or ever."

"Or ever." She lifted her hand for a high-five and he responded. The clap of their hands was loud and sharp.

"Come on," he said. "Let's get indoors and warm up. It's going to rain later. I'll make some coffee and we can get started."

"You think it's going to rain?"

"When is it not going to rain?"

"Funny. Hey, also, I just remembered. Red said that he wanted to see you." Calie did a fair imitation of Red's voice. "'Send him my way if he decides to show up'. Red might be mad?"

Brent glanced at the terminal building. Red's office was up in the top corner with a good view of both the runway and the public parking lot.

"All right," Brent said. "It's probably nothing. Why don't you open the reports we need and we'll line them up and get real methodical."

"You bet."

Brent started toward the terminal building, but looked over at Calie.

"Thanks," he said. "You might be over the top, but it's good having you damp me down a little. Or cheer me up."

"Did you know that it's in the job description? 'Keep Brent from getting too maudlin'. That's the actual word they use in there. 'Maudlin'. Sounds like a musical instrument. I had to look it up. Truly."

Brent smiled. "You're a riot. You should be on the stage."

"I know! Now hurry along. I can't do these reports without you."

Chapter Twenty-Two

The Candleton City Hall's doors still weren't open and it was a little after 10AM. The sign on the front said that the hours ran from *9.30AM until 4.45PM*.

Alicia was ready to bust down the doors.

Sitting around with David going over the documents had only made her madder.

As she knocked, harder than necessary, a portly security guard came out from a side door.

"Hey," he said. "Take it easy. They'll be open soon."

"How can it still be shut up?" Alicia said. "Look at the time."

"You're from out of town?"

"Yes."

"Well, they'll be open soon. Kind of how it works some days."

"Really? They send us this—" Alicia shook her fistful of documents "—and just make us stand around and wait."

"I just mind the door, ma'am."

Probably specifically because of people behaving like her.

"Well," David said, a little too philosophically, "it is Alaska."

"That it is, sir," the guard said. He scratched at the side of his face.

"All right," Alicia said. "We can watch the door from there."

She pointed to the café across the road where she and Brent had stopped the previous evening. David's little white rental car was parked right out front.

"Good," David said. "I could use a real coffee."

The same waitress was working. Shiron? No, Cheyenne. Her fine ginger hair was down today and had swept across her name badge.

"You have a new man already?" she said to Alicia. "You are chewing through them, honey."

"This is my brother," Alicia said.

The café hummed with people, and the air was just burgeoning with the delicious scents of pastries and fried food.

Cheyenne looked David up and down. "Your brother huh? Is he single?"

"Way too old for you," David said, holding up his hand and waggling his ring finger to show his wedding band.

"Copy that," Cheyenne said. "Coffee? Danish? Bagel?

Salmon sandwich? Pumpkin spice spirulina soy latte? I can take your order right here."

"Thanks," Alicia said. "Flat white please."

"You bet. Adventurous." Cheyenne looked at Brent, somehow making her eyes gooey at him.

Brent didn't even notice.

"Espresso," he said. "Double shot."

"We can do that. To eat?"

"We ate," Alicia said.

"Ah, well. Another time." Cheyenne took David's proffered twenty and slipped away behind the counter.

"It's like you're a regular here," David said, looking around for a table. Most of them were unoccupied and Alicia headed for the same one she and Brent had used yesterday. Right by the window, so it was a good spot to watch the city hall's doors.

Alicia found herself drumming her fingers on the table as they waited. David just leaned back in his chair.

"What if one of us moved in?" he said.

"Moved in?" she said.

"To Dad's house."

"Move in, like permanently?"

"Yes."

"By 'one of us', you mean me."

David shrugged.

"Because you *have a life*, right? A family and job that needs you."

"I'm just tossing ideas into the pan here."

Or trying to start another fight.

Alicia leaned her elbows on the table, and her chin in her hands.

"What?" David said

"Why are we even attached to the house? I mean, we didn't grow up here. We have no connection to the place. Dad's only been up here, what, twelve years? Thirteen?"

"You don't even know?"

"It's not as if we ever stayed in touch."

"Not one of his strengths."

"Well, not one of mine either."

"Apples and the distance from the tree, right?"

"You know it." She hated to admit that there were things about her father that she saw in herself. A certain stand-offishness. A quick temper. A tendency to focus on things to the exclusion of other things.

Aspects of herself that she didn't necessarily like, but she couldn't blame him. Like any parent, he'd done the best he could. As long has he'd been around. And she was getting better with the temper thing, and the ability to focus actually helped her with dealing with the complexities of contracts and the implications of them.

A pity she couldn't focus in like that on the house demolition order.

An order which didn't make any sense.

Why demolish a perfectly good house? It might be aging a little, and in need of a some maintenance, but knocking it down was extreme.

Cheyenne arrived with their coffees and a wink for David. He just smiled at her. She put the change on the table.

"That girl's going to get herself in trouble," Alicia said, picking up her cup. The coffee was delicious.

"Most likely," David said. "But it's good having her around."

"What?"

"You've calmed down a bit."

"Yeah."

"But you've started thinking about that guy again. Brent?"

"I haven't started thinking about him again," Alicia said, with a half-smile. "I haven't stopped." She took a gulp of the coffee and spluttered as some drips went down the wrong way.

"Take it easy," David said.

"I'm fine. I'm fine."

"You're not. You're smitten. Or worse. This is like a crush."

"Not at all. A crush is when you like someone, and fantasize about them, but you've never spoken to them."

"No," David said. "You can have talked to them. Just that you have feelings for them, but the other person is oblivious."

"Did he look oblivious to you?"

"No. Fair point."

And then she was right back there in her father's house. At the bottom of the stairway.

Brent's lips on hers.

A shiver ran through her.

"Am I hopeless?" she said.

"Something like that." David picked up his little cup and

downed his espresso in two gulps. "Come on. The doors are open."

Alicia looked and saw someone go into the City Hall, through the front doors.

"Let's go take care of this." She took another sip of her coffee and set the cup down.

David left a generous tip and gave Cheyenne a wave as they left. Cheyenne grinned back.

"What does Francine think about you flirting with wait-resses?" Alicia said as they crossed the street.

"Doesn't bother her. She's French."

"Oh, get over yourself. A middle-aged man ogling a–"

"I wasn't ogling. I was just being friendly. You should try that sometime."

"I'm friendly."

"Like a porcupine."

"Ouch. That stings. You know I'm grieving the loss of my father."

"I heard." David smiled.

The banter was good. Sure there was an edge to it, but it was keeping them close. Siblings. Kind of how it should be.

The Candleton City Hall's interior was stark and brood-ing. Like something out of Orwell. A high-ceiling in the living room-sized foyer, with stiff lines of tiles across the floor and single desk in one corner. Unoccupied.

Closed doors hid other parts of the building.

"There's a bell," David said, tapping a simple steel call bell on the desk. The chiming sound rang around the space.

"Just a moment," someone called from behind one of the doors. "Right with you."

"Small towns," David said. "You'd think I'd be used to this."

"Where are you living now?"

"Avenhead. Population eight hundred and six. Eight hundred and five while I'm up here. That's an Avenhead joke."

"I got. Not much of a sense of humor down that way?"

"Nope."

"And what is it you do for a living now?"

"Same old. Keep the state running. Keep the politicians honest." David had always been opinionated, and his little one-man outfit as a blogger, and now podcaster, seemed very fringe and a very marginal way to make a living. But the money came in, apparently. Subscriptions and sponsorships and guest appearances. A minor celebrity in Pontotoc County.

"You're doing all right?" Alicia said.

"Last year was lousy, but Francine does substitute teaching, so we did okay. This year's been amazing. Great things happening in politics and some people like my opinions. More than usual really."

"I don't want to know."

He grinned. "Yeah, you really don't."

With a clunk, followed by a creaking of stiff hinges, one of the doors opened and a middle-aged woman appeared. She had big glasses and streaks of pink in her blonde hair. She smiled at them.

"I'm Rosie," she said. "Like the name on the desk. Can I help."

A little upright plaque on the desk's front edge had her name engraved. There were papers spread across the desk, and an aging computer and a three-high set of plastic document trays.

"You want to bulldoze our father's house," Alicia said. "But if you try it, I'm going to be inside."

"Oh, dear." Rosie put both hands to her collarbone. Not mocking, but quite genuine.

"My thoughts exactly," David said.

Rosie went around behind her desk. "You're up on Bondurant Street, right? Near Ash."

Alicia gave the address.

"Yes." Rosie sat and tapped at her computer keyboard. The waving, swirling screensaver vanished and a login box came up. "You're going to need to speak with Bob." Rosie typed in her password.

"Bob?"

"Bob McGinley. He's in charge of all of that. We're putting in a new park there. The area needs it."

"You're putting in condos," Alicia said.

"That can't be right." Rosie typed some more and moused her way around the display.

"I have it here," Alicia said, holding up the documents. "Condominiums."

"We hardly need condos in Candleton," Rosie said, looked at them, tilting her head so she was looking over her glasses like an old-school librarian. "We have plenty of space. Plenty of housing."

"Tell that to the developers. Who probably have the mayor in their pockets."

"Not the mayor. Bob. He's a pushover. I have to breathe shallow when I'm around him so I don't accidentally blow him down."

David laughed. Alicia frowned at him.

"Sweetest guy," Rosie said. "But he's *too* nice. Just bows down to everyone. Sure does know infrastructure though."

"Sounds great," David said. "We need someone just like that."

"You do. I see here that you're right. Six condos spread over three property lots. How come I didn't know about that all? I'm going to need to speak with him. I'm on the front line here, I need to know all that."

"Can we talk to him?" Alicia said.

"Well, no. Bob's down in Anchorage having a procedure." Rosie rubbed her chin. "Won't be back until after the weekend. You could talk with Courtney. Let me give her a try."

"Courtney?"

"She's the parks and gardens person. She might know something about it. We're a smaller staff here. You're from out of town, aren't you?" Rosie peered at the screen. "Alicia and David? You're Nathan Brooks's children. Managing the... estate. Oh my. I am so sorry for your loss. This must be a terrible time for you."

"Pretty terrible," David said. "We're barely holding it together. Going through his stuff. It's devastating. And you can imagine the news that you want to run a wrecking ball through our lives is leaving us distraught and fragile."

"Oh my."

Alicia suppressed a smile. That was some performance. Made it sound as if they were a close-knit family and that their father's death had suddenly ripped their lives apart.

"Let's talk to Courtney, then," Alicia said. "At least we can get the ball rolling. *Not* the wrecking ball."

"You bet." From a corner of the desk, Rosie picked up a headset with a mic. She slipped it over her head, still mousing around the computer. She watched the display a moment.

"Holly?" she said into the headset's mic. "It's Rosie out front. Hey we have some people need to speak with Courtney. It's kind of urgent."

Rosie listened.

"Oh," she said after a moment. "Okay then. This afternoon? Tomorrow? Oh. I see. Well, I will be having words with her. I need to know these things. All right. Are we still on for coffee at three?"

Rosie smiled at Alicia and David.

"All right, Holly. See you then." Rosie clicked her mouse and pulled off the headset.

"Problem?" David said.

"Well, it turns out that Courtney booked herself in for some emergency management training and is out of the office today and tomorrow."

"So who's next in the chain there?" Alicia said.

"Nobody. Me?"

"Someone above Bob? The city manager?"

Rosie sighed. "In theory, yes. John would be the one to speak with. But that's not where his head is. He's not going to countermand someone on the staff. He's just going to say to wait until Bob returns. It's his area of expertise, after all."

"When's Bob going to be back?" Alicia said. "Because we sure could use some answers here before the bulldozers show up."

"She said already," David said. "After the weekend."

"Probably," Rosie said. "I mean it's a personal matter, so I can't divulge anything about it, but it might be a little longer.

"Longer," Alicia said.

Rosie shrugged. "I wish I could be more specific."

"Perhaps you could contact Bob," David said. "Just ask him a couple of questions."

"Sorry." Rosie held her hands up, splayed but with her wrists pressed together. "My hands are tied."

"I understand that," Alicia said. "But not so much for Courtney. This is urgent, as you yourself said."

"Right," David said. "I assume she's taking her training here in town. We could head around there and talk to her."

"Interrupt her training?" Rosie said.

"Dead right," Alicia said.

Rosie leaned back in her seat.

"How about this," she said. "I'll leave a message, and get Courtney to contact you directly when she's on a break?"

"Fair compromise," Alicia said. It felt like progress, even if it was incremental. Alicia said her phone number, and Rosie typed it into her computer, then typed some more.

"Message sent," she said. "Is than an Oklahoma number?"

"Yes," Alicia said.

"Long way from home."

"We really are," David said.

"Courtney should be in touch soon. But look, if she isn't, feel free to call me and I'll see if I can hurry things along."

From a caddy on the desk, Rosie took a business card. She laid it flat on the desk, crossed out something, and wrote her name in, then passed the card over.

"My predecessor left under a cloud in a hurry and they'd just gotten her two hundred fifty cards, so I'm stuck with them, crossing out her name and adding in mine. Phone number is the same."

"Thanks," Alicia took the card. "We'll be in touch."

They headed out and drove back to Bondurant Street, to find a crane, a backhoe and a giant semi with a huge flat-tray parked out front of the house two along from their father's place. Workers were busy jacking the house there up.

"They're already starting," David said. "We're not going to be able to fight this."

"That's what they think."

"Alicia, please." David parked across the road.

"Nope," she said. "Don't talk to me like that. I'm going to have words. And you'd better be backing me up."

"Of course," he said. "Of course."

It was reassuring that he didn't even hesitate.

Alicia opened her door and stepped out of the little car.

Chapter Twenty-Three

Red Dalton's airport manager office sported big framed black and white photographs of World War Two aircraft. A squadron of Lightnings, a Liberator in cloud, a pair of Flying Fortresses on a runway, and a glistening, silvery Superfortress high over the desert.

Red wasn't there. So much for wanting to see Brent.

Then again, Red had a whole bunch of different roles to play in the city. His own little bookstore open two days a week, and not really turning a profit, duties as the deputy mayor, and working as the airport manager. To be fair, the bookstore was staffed, and he only dropped by from time to time to have some oversight, but still.

Brent wandered out of the office onto the mezzanine balcony that looked out of the terminal's concourse. Small as airports went, but it was still one of the fanciest buildings in

Wilkes Landing, with wood paneling and new seating. The clocks on the wall were actually a little disconcerting. A community like this, time was generally less of an issue.

Still, airports seemed to have their own ecosystems.

Seattle airport–Sea-Tac–had been like a little city. A bit overwhelming for a boy from the heart of Alaska. The whole trip had been. Tens of thousands of people at the concert, brilliant lights and blasting music.

Imagine LA or NYC or Chicago. LAX, JFK or O'Hare in Chicago. Airports with multiple terminals and multiple runways. Hundreds upon hundreds of people on their fire crews.

There were a few people around below Brent on the terminal's maroon and teal checked carpet tile floor. A few travelers, Bree with cart parked out front of the public toilets, reloading the toilet paper, and Mitch and Candace at the check-in counter. Despite the incident, people still had places to be and schedules to keep.

"Hey up there!" Red called from floor, appearing through the door through to the baggage sorting area. He waved at Brent. Red was wearing a black sports jacket and jeans. Probably not many deputy mayors and airport managers could get away with that kind of casual look.

"Should I come down?" Brent said.

"I'll be right up." Red headed for the stairway.

The second level of the terminal had the offices, a token lounge–little more than a living room, with a coffee machine and a little soda fridge–and some storage. It was almost as if

Wilkes Landing wanted to be bigger and more sophisticated. But it was always going to be a backwater. Amazing really, that it had an airport at all.

"Well," Red said, reaching the second floor and coming along. He held his hand out to shake, which was a little unusual. Probably still smarting from the incident.

Brent took Red's hand and they shook. Red clapped him on the right shoulder.

"You did us proud," Red said.

"I did my job."

"And still."

"And it was all Calie. She deserves the credit."

"She does. She's an asset to us for sure. I hope we don't lose her to S.A.R."

"Well, we all moonlight."

"Yes we do, yes we do."

"She said you wanted to see me."

Red sighed. "I've had questions, you see."

"Uh-huh. Questions. About what?"

"Come into the office."

Brent followed him in, and Red gestured for him to take a seat across the desk. Outside a squall had blown in and was racing in across the tarmac. A hazy wall of rain.

"Closing the airport?" Brent said. It wasn't so infrequent that they had to close for an hour or two. Usually there was plenty of warning, so flights were delayed before they left the ground, rather than having to find alternative airports while en route.

"Nah," Red said, twiddling with a pen. "This is going to be gone in twenty minutes." He leaned forward, with his elbows on the desk.

"Something up?" Brent said.

"I've got the DOT asking questions."

"Of course." The Alaska Department of Transportation and Public Facilities would of course want to get all the details. "I have a five foot stack of reports to fill in back at the fire house. We should have it done in a week. Ten days at the outside. It's a lot of paperwork."

"Yes. Imagine if the event had been worse."

"I try not to." Not so much for the extra paperwork, but for the people involved.

"Yes," Red said. "So, there is a specific question." He leaned back.

"Oh? And that is?" It wasn't like Red to beat around the bush.

"Your license."

"My license?"

"Your Air Operations Area Ramp License has expired."

"No it hasn't." The license allowed him to drive vehicles on the airport. Technically on the AOA–the Air Operations Area.

"Expired two years ago."

There was a computer on Red's desk and he turned the display toward Brent. With a few clicks of the mouse, Red brought up an email. He opened the attachment.

Brent's license document. With an expiry more than two years ago.

"It's a mistake," Brent said.

"That may well be, but I can't let you drive on the apron or anywhere until it's resolved." Red turned and peered out across the tarmac. "I can't even let you drive your pickup from where it's parked, back to the entry. Someone will have to do it for you."

"Now?" Brent said. "This comes up now? And until it's resolved, I've got to, what, park in the public lot and walk to the fire house?" It wasn't as if he was averse to walking five hundred yards or so, but it felt like just some clerical error.

"It comes up now because there was an incident. It looks bad for us, to have an unlicensed fire chief cruising around the tarmac in a big old Oshkosh when there are aircraft movements. Worse than just looks bad, it's a breach of regulations."

Now Brent leaned back, kind of dumbfounded.

"It's a clerical error," Brent said. "Someone's just tapped the wrong key when they've reissued the license."

Red blew air through pursed lips.

"It's just a glitch," Brent said. "One phone call can fix it. Why does it expire anyway? I'm always in training. Always out on the apron anyway."

"I know it. You know it. Calie knows it. Even the board knows it. You're the best aviation chief in Alaska. At least, in small town Alaska."

"Thanks, I think."

"And yet, if something were to happen, while you were unlicensed, the liability would be ridiculous. People's lives are at stake."

Brent rolled his shoulders. He knew that. The very reason

he was a fire fighter was to save lives, wasn't it? And yet some broken bureaucracy was now getting in the way.

"So what happens now?" Brent said. "You call Anchorage and take care of it? Get the error taken care of."

"They'll need documentation. You might have to dig it out."

"They should have it all."

"'Should have it all' doesn't mean 'does have it all'."

"Sheesh."

"I called you up here since I didn't want for you to get started on your reports on the incident and run across this cold."

"Right."

Red leaned forward again. "Brent, I'm eternally grateful to have you as a member of the team here, but you know as well as me that the aviation industry runs on regulations. You look at what's happened over recent years when people have taken shortcuts. It's not like we're running a library, now it is. We have heavy machinery worth millions of dollars moving at hundreds of miles an hour. With fragile human bodies inside."

Brent gave a nervous laugh. It was one way of putting it, perhaps.

"Let's go for a drink tonight," Red said. "Lobster Lodge happy hour from seven until eight. How about that? I'll buy the first round."

"You don't need to do that." Brent stood. "Let me get to work on the reports and see if I can't just get into the system and get this license issue straightened out."

"Or you could take a couple of days. Go toss a hook in the

water up at Milverton Pond. You might get yourself a whopper." Red held his arms as wide as he could, indicating how big of a fish Brent might land.

"I might just, but after. First, you know, we need to expedite these reports. Already I feel guilty for not being around yesterday afternoon."

"You weren't around?"

Brent smiled "Yep, that's how important I am around here."

"Are you mad?"

"Not much. Just, well, disappointed. As you say, the aviation industry has to be careful. Every 't' needs its cross and every 'i' needs its dot. People's lives in our hands. And yet some clerical error is keeping me from doing my job."

"We'll get it sorted out real soon. Before you know it."

"I'm sure. Anything else?"

"Nope. Just, well, thanks for doing a great job. It's reassuring to me knowing that you're right there and ready."

"Thanks." Brent headed for the door. "I'll let you know about tonight. Depends of these reports, I guess."

"I know it. Talk to you later."

Back out on the terminal's mezzanine balcony. There were more people around now, and a light passenger aircraft was pulling up on the apron right in front of the building Mitch and Candace were busy at the counter, checking people in for the next flight.

Brent headed out, walking the path along the fence from the terminal back to the fire house. The air was cold, cutting in around his neck. Ernie's chopper was just taking to the air, the thrashing of the rotors loud across the tarmac and off the surrounding hills. In moments, the aircraft was high and turning, heading south.

"Hey," Calie said when Brent stepped into the fire house's cozy office. She was sitting at her desk, staring into the computer display, eyes looking glazed. "Are you in trouble for bailing yesterday morning? And coming in late today?"

"Red barely noticed." Brent explained about the license problem. There was coffee in the kitchen nook, and a little box of donuts on the bench.

"So you're walking, I guess?" Calie said. "How are you going to get back up to Candleton for your next date?"

"Helicopter." Brent selected an unfrosted donut and took a bite. Way too sweet.

"Ow, yes!" Calie said. "It must be great to have Ernie Williams as a buddy."

"It is. But I'm kidding. I'm not taking a helicopter up to Candleton." It would be nice, though. He would be there in something like twenty minutes. "Besides Ernie has just headed away."

"He'll be back. I could drive you up there, I suppose. I know you don't think much of my driving, but—"

"Your driving is fine."

"—think of the fun we could have."

"So much fun. I'm not going back up to Candleton." Much as he would like to. "And I haven't lost my driver's license, just my Ramp License."

"Right, yes, you said. Your Air Operations Area Ramp License. You can't drive on airport property."

"Exactly. I'll even need you to move my pickup from in front of the fire house, to just outside the gate."

"Seriously? Is that how retentive it's getting now?"

"Apparently."

"All right," Calie said, standing from her desk. "I'm making little headway here. Some of the questions are contradictory, and some of them are just repetitions of other questions. And then you've got to fill out a different form for another agency, but it's all the same information, but you can't save as you go and you can't copy-paste and you can't flip between tabs, since it just blanks whatever you'd typed in the first place. I need a coffee." She headed for the kitchen nook.

Brent pulled around another office chair and parked it next to Calie's.

The pages on the display were dense. Lots of legalese, perhaps. Surely they should make this as easy to do as possible.

"When was the last time we had an incident?" Calie said. "Was that about two months ago when the wheel popped off old Manny Crenshaw's Cessna and he put it through the fence?"

"That was the one." Manny tended to get a little light on the maintenance. Figured that if he died he wasn't going to have any passengers so what did it matter? Brent had pointed out numerous times that it could matter. *Search and rescue for your body Manny, what about that? People who would rather just be at home in front of the fire.*

"So when are you seeing her again?" Calie said. "Alicia."

"Didn't we talk about this?"

"We did, but that was forty-five minutes ago. I figure you've been back and forth with her with dozens of texts."

"Nothing."

"She must have texted you." Calie came back over, carrying a fresh coffee and a glazed donut.

"No," Brent said. "She hasn't. I think that both of us know that it was nothing."

That kiss though. He could still feel her lips on his.

"Maybe your phone's broken." Calie set the coffee and donut on the desk. "Let me take a look."

"At what?"

"Your phone, bozo. Quickly."

With a sigh, Brent handed it over.

"Pin."

Brent told her the number.

Calie tapped at the display.

"Alicia B.'," she said.

"Yuh."

"'Miss you'. You texted her that you miss her? That's so sweet."

"Long story." Brent explained about handing his phone to Alicia, actually keeping the story short.

"Hmm," Calie said. "And she hasn't texted back yet."

"Nope. There you go."

"Well, I imagine she's busy, what with the estate from her father. And her brother on the scene."

Calie tapped at the phone's display with her thumbs.

"What are you doing?" Brent said.

"Sending her a text."

"Please don't."

"You're going to like it."

Brent held his hand out.

Calie took a step back. She kept tapping.

"There." She passed the phone to him. "I typed it, but I didn't send it. That's over to you, loverboy."

Brent read the unsent text.

I hope things are going smoothly with your bro and taking care of the house. Had a great time hanging with you. Hope we can do it again sometime.

Brent kept looking at the words. Friendly, really. Innocent. Calie knew what she was doing.

"Oh, don't just stare at it. Send it."

"I don't know."

"Oh, boy! Give it to me. I'll send it."

"Right."

"I don't get why you're so nervous. Obviously she likes you."

Obviously. That kiss.

"I know," Brent said. "And I like her. But it's complicated. She's grieving her father. Wading into that is like–"

"Oh, cut it out. Does that text read as if it's wading into something? It's just being friendly. She could use a friend, don't you think?"

"Yes." Brent tapped on the text.

"What are you doing? Changing it?"

"Just changing 'your bro' to his name. David."

"Smart."

"That's me."

"Don't fool yourself."

Brent tapped to send the text. The phone made a quiet chime.

"Done," he said.

"Good work. Now I guess we can focus on these reports."

"Great." As Brent pocketed his phone, it chimed.

Calie grinned. "You're welcome," she said.

"Yeah, yeah. It's probably just a fishing buddy."

But it wasn't. It was Alicia.

I had a great time too.

But that was all.

"Busy, I guess," Calie said, looking over Brent's shoulder. "But it's a start. It's a good sign that she texted back right away."

Brent didn't want to think about it. The whole thing was just impossible.

Though didn't people like Red often say that the impossible just takes longer.

He felt on the cusp of something. Felt like he should just get in his pickup and drive back up there. He'd probably wind up looking like a fool, but at least he wouldn't be sitting around moping. Wondering what might have happened.

But there were reports to do.

"Let's get this done fast," he said. "Then maybe I can..."

"Maybe you can what?" Calie said with a grin.

"Maybe see if she wants to see me."

Calie punched his shoulder. "Attaboy."

Chapter Twenty-Four

Alicia sat on the veranda of her father's house. The sun was bright, but the air was still cool. It was kind of warmer than she'd expected. In her head, Alaska was essentially just one big fridge-freezer, iced in for most of the year.

From along the street came the clanks and whirrs and hums of the team working on the house removal. Sometimes loud, sometimes quiet. Sometimes so quiet she wondered if they had stopped work entirely.

The place was the one she'd noticed the previous evening, and promptly forgotten. The house without the trees, and with the eviction notice on the door. Except it wasn't an eviction notice. It was a demolition notice. Even though they weren't demolishing it. They were jacking it up, loading it on a truck and it was getting driven away to other locations.

She's spoken to the foreman. They would work through

the day to get the house loaded onto the big flat tray, and after nightfall, they would drive the house away.

"The town's streets are quieter after dark," he'd said. "It makes road management easier."

The house was bound for a place called Teakball. A tiny mining outpost two hundred miles north, where they needed buildings and were getting desperate.

As if that mattered.

The point was that already the city was going ahead and clearing the block. The foreman had told her that two other places were already vacant and ready to go, but that there were holdouts, people who were determined to not relinquish their homes.

"I understand that," Alicia had said.

The foreman had nodded sympathetically, but he was just doing his job.

Alicia had walked around the block, seeing people's homes and lives. Houses a similar age to her father's place, with clapboard exterior walls and tiled roofing. Little garden plots and dreamcatchers hanging from the veranda frames. A child's tricycle. A trampoline. Curtains pulled back, with fireplaces and big televisions and wall art inside. SUVs in the driveways.

It could have been suburban Tulsa.

Well, except for the mountains surrounding the town. They stood there, blue and brooding. Kind of like her mood really.

And it was more than the mountains. It was the brilliant crispness in the air. The low angle of the sun. The general

background sound of town. It was odd, but it felt *friendlier*.
Neighbors talking with each other. People helping out.

Even if the city was taking away houses to put up condos.

As Alicia sat there, her phone chimed with a text.

From Brent.

I hope things are going smoothly with David, and taking care of the house. Had a great time hanging with you. Hope we can do it again sometime.

That made her smile. Lifted her spirits.

Nothing too overt. No mention of the extraordinary kiss they'd shared. She was still trembling from it. At least, on the inside.

She started tapping in.

I had a great time too. And I really hope that we can do it again soon. You're a little shining light here for me. P.S. That kiss was amazing.

She was about to send it when she heard the creak of the front door behind, and a footfall on the veranda.

She didn't turn.

"Hello?" David said. The door creaked again as he closed it. "I wondered where the hang you'd gotten to."

"I went for a walk."

"Yeah."

"This whole block is going."

"I know."

"Some of the other places are already empty."

"Do we care?"

"I feel this hollow in the pit of my stomach. It's like everything on the same day. I get that we have no attachment to the house, but for the fact that our father lived her. I would just have liked a little longer before they arrived with the jacks and the backhoe and the massive hauler truck ready to take the place away."

"I talked to the foreman for a moment," David said. "After you stormed off."

"I didn't storm off."

"You left partway through a conversation, and you walked with purpose off along the sidewalk."

"Clearing my head." Alicia looked around. "Did I offend him?"

David snorted. "That guy? It would take a whole lot more than a woman storming off to offend him."

"I didn't storm off."

"Jus' razzing ya sis."

She smiled.

David sat next to her and stared off across the street.

"It just feels rushed," she said. "I would have liked a couple of weeks, you know. Just to look through his things. To reminisce a little. Relax into it."

"Don't you need to get back for work?"

"Sure. But... I can hotspot my phone and do a whole

bunch online anyway." She could have even flown back for a meeting or two, and come back to Alaska.

Except that it took a whole day to get here. And the last time she'd flown it hadn't gone so well.

"It's going to be all right," David said. "We'll talk to Courtney. Or Bob. Or both. Even with the removal orders, yada-yada, they're not going to jack up the house tomorrow."

"Oh, I understand that. But it's there. Hanging over my head."

"Right."

Alicia stood. Took a breath. The air was so crisp and clear and cool. And the setting was spectacular. No wonder their father had chosen this as a place to settle.

"Let's get started anyway," she said, looking back at the old house. "'Trash', 'donate' and 'to decide'."

"Three boxes. Like a decluttering project?"

"You got it."

"There you are. Solutions-focused as always."

Alicia laughed. "That's me."

"I suppose at least there's not going to be anything sentimental. We might not even need your 'to decide' box."

"Nope, we might not."

"After all," David said, with a wink, "you've got enough decisions in your life right now."

"Meaning what?"

"Meaning that guy. Brent. Big decisions there."

"You nut. There's nothing to decide there. He lives in Wilkes Landing. I live in Tulsa. I met him less than forty-eight hours ago."

"When you know, you know."

"When I know what? You are starting to bug me."

"Not when you know. When I know. I saw the two of you together. I see the way you've been acting since he headed away."

"How have I been acting?"

"Distant. Pining. Quick to flare."

"Whatever. Anyway, how would you know? We never spend any time together. You have no idea what I'm like day to day."

"Pretty sure it's not this."

"I'm not pining. Anything you see about me is all about Dad's passing."

David gave a soft smile and he nodded. "Okay then. Let's go get on with this."

He turned and stepped back up the veranda. Went inside.

But Alicia stayed on the step for a moment longer, listening to the sounds of machinery from two houses along.

She was never going to admit it to David, but really she was pining.

Brent had been in the back of her mind all day. Like some ridiculous schoolgirl crush. Just as David had said.

And then the text she'd been about to send.

Smitten. Shot by cupid's arrow. Falling for him.

She read it over.

I had a great time too. And I really hope that we can do it again soon. You're a little shining light here for me. P.S. That kiss was amazing.

. . .

What was she thinking?

Just like that. It was all so twee and silly. The big strong fire fighter cliché. Thank goodness she hadn't sent it.

She tapped to backspace across most of it. When she did tap to send, all that she'd left was,

I had a great time too.

That was enough. She didn't need to mire herself in something, no matter how tempting.

And this man was very tempting.

She just about started tapping again in the words she'd deleted.

Instead, she just tapped 'Send'.

"I need to talk to Melissa," Alicia whispered to herself. "Where men are concerned she could talk anyone down from the ledge."

Melissa had been through two nasty divorces and now had a collection of barge poles with which to keep men at bay. Attractive and coy, men circled her, she said, like bees around pansies or cornflowers.

Part of Alicia was envious of that capacity Melissa had, to snap her fingers and have males falling over themselves to do her bidding, but there was a whole lot that came with that.

Way too much attention and way too much of that inappropriate.

Too often she felt like she couldn't go out alone, felt like she couldn't dress up, felt as if she needed to carry a Taser.

The machinery fell silent for a moment, and a pickup drove by on the street.

Alicia didn't look. She just stepped up onto the veranda and went inside to call Melissa.

Chapter Twenty-Five

Brent finished up with the first tranche of the reports on the incident. It seemed these days as if every agency needed some paperwork. The airport itself. Alaska Fire and Rescue. The aircraft's manufacturer. Department of Fish and Game. Where they fitted into it was anyone's guess.

He sat back and looked out through the office's small window. His pickup was still parked out there. He had to remember to get Calie to shift it for him.

Part of him knew that it would be fine to just drive it himself. It was only a matter of fifty yards or so. He'd been driving for almost two decades with barely more than a scrape. That was saying something in Alaska.

But then, of course, inevitably, if he did get behind the wheel while the pickup was on private airport property, more than likely something would happen. Nothing like driving into an aircraft. Probably just bumping the fence or running a tire off the concrete onto the grass.

And the outcome would be worse than just more paper-work. He'd likely be suspended from his job, if not fired. And poor Red would have to face more questions from the depart-ment and other officials. Essentially over a clerical error.

Brent sighed.

"You're thinking about her, aren't you," Calie said from her desk. She didn't even look up.

"Constantly," Brent said. "I'm considering stealing Ernie's chopper and flying up there."

"You don't know how to fly a chopper."

"How hard can it be? Start the engine and point the stick wherever you want to go. It's not like I'm going encounter logging trucks and elk up in the air, right?"

"You think you're being funny, but it strikes me that you're feeling adrift without her. Your life has lost direction. That's why you're considering desperate measures like thieving your friend's whirlybird."

"You have me pegged."

Calie was leaning back in her office chair, with a cup of some kind of spirulina seaweed beet mix of indeterminate color.

"How about this?" Calie said. "When we're done here, I'll move your pickup off airport property for you, but I'll move it all the way to Bondurant Street in Candleton. You can either come with, or just pick it up later."

"Bondurant Street? How do you know that?"

"Oh, please. I'm sitting here in front of a computer all day. You think that I'm not going to get the deets on your girlfriend."

Brent was tired of arguing. Calie was just using the word to get a rise out of him.

"No response?" Calie said.

"Nothing that won't come right back and bite me."

"I've got her socials here, if you wanted to take a look. Best friends with Olivia and Melissa. Brother is called–"

"Just stop. That's prying."

"I'm doing it for you."

"You're not helping. If things are meant to be, then something will happen. I wouldn't help my case by stalking her online."

Interesting. Where had that come from? *If things are meant to be.* Hadn't he already given up on it? Usually flings lasted a couple of days, rather than a single kiss, but he could satisfy himself with that.

Couldn't he?

"Hello," Calie said. "Earth to Brent."

"What?"

"You got kind of glazed there for a moment."

"I guess I did. I know her brother is David. I met him."

"There you are."

"And it was best to just butt out and leave them to get on with taking care of their father's house."

Calie just stared at him.

"How are the reports coming?" Brent said.

"Reports?" Calie glanced at her computer display. "I've

done all I can. I think you need to take care of some parts. Then we can hand them all on to Red for his final say-so."

Brent leaned forward on his desk and scrolled through the report he was working on. Almost done. They were making surprisingly good progress.

"What's the time?" he said.

"Look in the bottom right of your computer screen, Brent."

"Ha, ha."

It was a little after one in the afternoon, which made him feel hungry.

"We should call for pizza," Calie said, as if reading his thoughts.

"Go ahead. I could eat." Donaldo's Italian down on Henshaw street offered afternoon delivery. "Extra cheese."

"You got it." Calie leaned into her computer again.

Others from the emergency crew stopped by to check in. Dan and Harrison and Mae. They'd done various jobs around the place—packing away gear and checking some inventory—to give Brent and Calie the chance to work on the reports.

But now the reports were almost done.

And Brent wasn't allowed to drive on airport property.

And Red had said he should take a couple of days. Get in some fishing.

A couple of days.

Brent took out his phone.

The text from Alicia.

. . .

I had a great time too.

He had a couple of days, if he wanted them. Maybe he could just 'happen' to be passing through Candleton. Maybe she might have time to meet for coffee.

Maybe he was dreaming.

I had a great time too.

Why did he keep reading over those six words? He should just put her out of his mind. Go fishing as Red had suggested.

"Half an hour," Calie said. "Hope you like anchovies."

"Love them."

"Oh. I was kidding. I hate them, so we've got no anchovies."

"Fine. How many times have we ordered pizza before?"

"Couple of dozen?"

"And we didn't know that about each other?"

"I'm sure we talk about it every time."

"I'm sure we don't."

Calie was grinning. "Did you text her back yet?"

"Just thinking about it."

He could. It didn't have to mean anything.

Wouldn't it be a bit obvious, though? The whole idea that he just happened to be passing through Candleton the very next day. Cheesy or corny or whatever.

"You need to be honest," Calie said.

"I know."

"Do you? I see you sitting there like you're practicing for a solo wrestling match. Get out in the thin branches. Life is nothing if it's not a bold risk."

"Where did you get that? Some book of Zen?"

"On the wrapper of a cherry throat lozenge."

Brent laughed.

He looked at his phone again.

I have a couple of days off, he tapped in. *Take you for coffee again?*

He backspaced it all out.

Clerical error means... he tapped in, then backspaced it all.

"Be decisive!" Calie said, watching him, clearly understanding how he was hesitating. "Imagine she's inside of a blazing plane and you need to charge in and carry her to safety."

I'm off for a couple of days, he tapped. *Fancy going for coffee again?*

He tapped send before he could change his mind.

Then he added another text.

I understand if you're overwhelmed with things.

"Attaboy," Calie said.

"You don't even know what I sent."

"Doesn't matter. The point is that you sent something."

Chapter Twenty-Six

It was after seven in the evening when Alicia finally looked at her phone.

She and David had spent the afternoon hauling things to the living room and dividing them among boxes. Unopened packs of pajamas and underwear, boxes with brand new shoes. A printer and a cordless drill. Packs of thirty black ballpoint pens.

"I can use the drill," Alicia had said as they filled the 'donate' box.

"Yeah," David had said. "And there are some unopened tube paints I'll take for Jake. He's been painting a whole lot."

"Wonderful."

They'd gone through the laundry, the kitchen and the spare room. The boxes were looking ready to go. They would need to get more.

Neither Alicia nor David were ready to tackle the junk

room. From the few times that Alicia had looked in, it seemed as if most of the stuff in it would be going to the landfill. Or recycling.

She sat in the living room, resting on one of the sofas, with her feet up on one of the corrugated cardboard boxes.

There were numerous texts on her phone. She'd set the thing to 'silent' so she could concentrate. Goodness knew that she spent much too much time on it anyway.

Olivia and Melissa, of course. Her boss. The guy who mowed her lawn. A reminder about her upcoming dental appointment. A couple of other friends.

And two from Brent.

Before she even thought about it, she'd tapped to open the texts.

I'm off for a couple of days. Fancy going for coffee again?

Then.

I understand if you're overwhelmed with things.

She was overwhelmed with things, but right away she found herself drifting to that moment in the foyer, just over there, where they'd kissed.

And she looked over the boxes of her father's detritus.

"My brain is mush," she murmured.

"I've known that for years," David said, coming in. "Are we on a break?"

"I am. You're not, I'm guessing."

"Hadn't occurred. My momentum is just getting up."

"Is momentum the thing we need? Shouldn't we take our time over this? Stop and ponder. Take the time to look through the old photo albums and the letters. I mean, he wrote actual letters, you know. Ink on paper and mailed in an envelope using the friendly facilities offered by the United States Postal Service."

"Obvious stuff first, of course. Are you sentimental about the unopened cordless drill? About the crockery that he clearly bought at Target in Anchorage?"

"Fair point."

David sat next to her. He smelled a little sweaty from working. A familiar, family scent. He glanced at her phone.

"You should go for it," he said.

"What?"

"This guy. You should be like a teenager and just enjoy it for what it is. At least it would be a counterpoint to all of this." David scratched at his neck. "This is going to get dull real quick."

"Only because you're trying to rush it."

"I don't want to *savor* it. We need to get it done. Take a little time for reminiscing, and a lot of time for bagging stuff up and getting it out the door."

Alicia rolled her shoulders. "I'm glad you're here," she said. "But—"

"But part of you wishes I'd never come."

"Not what I was going to say."

"But you're thinking it. I got in the way of your little tryst. And now I'm bringing organization to cleaning this all up."

"It wasn't a little tryst. It was like that old Pink Floyd album title."

"*The Dark Side of the Moon?* Or *Meddle?*"

"Trust you to know some obscure album. I mean *A Fragmentary Loss of Reason*, of course."

"*Momentary*. It's *A Momentary Lapse of Reason*."

Alicia smiled at him.

"Oh! You got me," he said. "You know the title."

"For sure. And for a momentary fragment of time, I lost reason. I got all heady and horny and lascivious."

"Too much information about my sister right there."

She grinned again. It was fun teasing him.

David looked at his wrist. He had a nice hefty sports watch. Analogue. One of the ones with an adjustable bezel and the time in three different zones, with a stopwatch built in. Probably waterproof to sixty fathoms.

"It is getting late," he said. "They're still working on the house down there."

Alicia had been out for air a couple of times, and taken a look at the progress. The house two along, where she'd talked to the foreman, had been jacked up and they'd backed the flatbed under it. Presumably they would lower the jacks and tie the house down to be ready to drive off at whatever time that was going to happen.

"Late, yes," she said. "Perhaps we should just break for the day. Get some food in us, and rest up. Probably should just watch a movie."

David sighed. "Yeah." He looked at his watch again. "I was hoping that we would hear from Courtney. Or Bob. You know, about the house."

"I know. I suppose we could go down and pound on the city hall doors again at nine thirty tomorrow morning?"

"I'm all for that."

"We should eat too."

"I'm done in for cooking, though," Alicia said. "Physically and mentally."

"Don't worry. I'll go get take out."

"In Candleton? Where there are three stores and the post office is barely more than a closet?"

"Funny. There are a couple of places. You want a sandwich? Like a hoagie?"

"A sub."

"Yeah, yeah. There's a little spot I saw on the way in from the airport. *Grinders, Heroes and Hoagies*. I think it's a joke. You know, we're about as far from New York and Philly as you can get."

"I know it."

"I'll be back in half an hour. Try not to get too carried away texting that man. And notice there that I didn't say 'boyfriend'."

"I noticed. Thanks for your remarkable powers of discretion."

"You bet." David patted his pockets for his rental car keys and his wallet.

"You're not even going to ask me what I would like?"

"Meatball with smoked cheese, chipotle sauce, no lettuce and no jalapeños. I doubt they even have jalapeños up here."

"But err on the side of caution. And I'm impressed that you would know that. However, I'm all grown up now, so how about something with shaved ham, lots of tomato and pepper and surprise me with the cheese and the sauce."

"Wow. So grown up. See you soon."

Then he was gone. Out into the cooling night.

Alicia took a look at her phone again.

I'm off for a couple of days, Brent had sent. *Fancy going for coffee again?*

I understand if you're overwhelmed with things.

She smiled.

Pretty overwhelmed, she typed in.

She tapped send.

Then she typed some more.

Coffee would be nice. I'll probably be around for a couple more days.

. . .

Send.

Don't feel obliged, though. It's a long way up here.

Send.

She set the phone aside. Went to the kitchen and drew herself a glass of water.

She realized that she was listening out for the phone's little chime. But it didn't come.

Well, he was probably busy. Maybe out with that Calie or someone else.

He'd said he was off for a couple of days. Perhaps he'd headed into the hills for hiking and fishing. Hadn't he mentioned something about liking that? Getting out of the town and into the wilderness?

When she sat back on the sofa, a new text had come in.

This is Alaska, he'd sent, *Distance is an illusion.*

That made her smile. She'd had a friend in college who'd come from Rhode Island. The distances in Oklahoma had made her goggle. A huge trip for her had been going into Hartford or Boston.

.   .   .

No illusion, she typed. *It took hours to get here.*

She sent it, then another.

Longer than it would take me to get from Tulsa to Dallas.

That was a stretch, but it hardly mattered.
   A moment later he replied.

You must be a reckless driver.

She was never reckless. Unless having this conversation counted. She was conservative and wary. She'd never even driven directly to Dallas. She'd been over to Oklahoma City on the turnpike a few times. Seventy-five miles an hour, and people were still speeding by her.

The worst, she sent back.

A moment later, he replied.

.   .   .

Are you reckless with other things?

A tingle ran through her.

Phone flirting. Was that even him texting her? Maybe Calie had gotten hold of his phone and was being his representative. Asking her if she was reckless didn't quite seem like the man she knew.

Right then, Alicia laughed. She didn't really know him. They'd talked a little on the drive up. Family stuff and Alaska stuff, but there had been many long, quiet stretches. Neither of them feeling that they needed to fill a silence.

Didn't they say if you could be comfortable in silence with someone, then that was a good sign? Didn't that usually apply to old friends though?

I can be reckless, she texted.

Then put the phone aside and stood and went to the front door.

She was being like a teenager. *Recklessly* texting with a good looking guy. It was so crazy impractical. Impossible.

In a few days she would be flying back to Tulsa. The estate tidied and settled.

Maybe the house would even have been carted away like the others to make way for the new condos.

Although, given what happened the last time she'd flown, perhaps she should drive home.

Standing on the veranda, she breathed in the sweet cool air. She shivered in the growing cold. The sky was growing streaked with gorgeous vermillion and crimson and pumpkin orange. Like the paints David would take home for Jake.

It was very nice here. She kept getting reminded why her father would have moved all this way. The isolation from his kids notwithstanding, at least he would have gotten to enjoy sunsets like this. Even if he would have been practically frozen in six months of the year.

A flicker of recognition of something herself shone gently in the back of her mind.

There was no urgency here. No rush to get a developer's signature. No racing from work to yoga to coffee with Olivia, then back to mind the kids for Melissa. No turnpike that seemed to double as a racetrack.

In fact, from where she was standing, the only way to drive back to Oklahoma led through Canada. Through the Yukon and British Colombia. Alaska was part of the *contiguous* United States—joined by land—but not part of the *continuous* United States—there was a country in between.

That separation felt good right now. The isolation felt good.

It felt like something she needed. The slow down.

Perhaps her father had known what he was doing, dying up here.

Alicia shivered again as the chill of night took hold. The colors through the clouds were deepening. Darkening.

She turned and went back inside to get things ready for whatever kind of dinner David brought home.

She looked at her phone, lying face down on the sofa cushion, and ignored it.

A force of will.

But it was as if her head was clearing, and she wasn't sure that getting back into texting with that gorgeous man was going to help.

Besides, she had all night.

Chapter Twenty-Seven

From his pokey little dining room, Brent watched the sky. Sunsets out here could take a long time. On his trips south, to Seattle and northern California and a few other stops, he'd been surprised by the way the sun seemed to vanish so quickly.

If it had been visible at all. The story was that it rained a lot in Alaska, but it sure had rained plenty in other places he'd been. On the couple of days of the trip to Seattle there had been enough rain for a month up in Wilkes Landing. The skies had only really cleared for the few hours of the concert, as if the band had some deal with the weather gods.

Brent was searing a slab of salmon, and roasting some vegetables. It felt good to cook after the day of mind-melting reports, and Calie's energetic company.

It had been fun to text back and forth briefly with Alicia, but he hadn't heard for a while now.

He couldn't expect to.

He'd texted *Are you reckless with other things?* and stared at the display after he'd sent it, feeling like he was the one being too reckless.

Flirting with her. Enjoying it.

But low-risk, of course. She was hours away in Candleton, the use of a helicopter notwithstanding. She was going back to Oklahoma.

It wasn't as if texting would lead anywhere.

Perhaps that was what was encouraging him to be reckless like that.

I can be reckless, she'd texted back.

Right away, he'd sent,

I'd like to see that.

Then wished that there was a way to recall a text.

But it was done. And she hadn't replied.

That had been a hour back.

Perhaps he'd overstepped the mark. Dork.

He served the meal and sat at his little table, reading over one of the Air Operations manuals. It was a binder with around four hundred pages of dense text. It was kind of geeky, but he tried to read a few pages a day. Just to ensure that he knew his way around. Kind of his responsibility to passengers and the airport.

In the light of the incident, he felt vindicated really.

The salmon was delicious, but a little overdone, and the vegetables were good–his mother's old recipe involving too much oil and too many herbs, but he'd gotten it right. There was enough that he'd loaded a second plate, wrapped in Saran and put it in the fridge to microwave tomorrow.

He found himself checking his phone as he read, and ate..

Even though it should chime when a text came in, he got paranoid that he'd left the 'Do Not Disturb' setting on, or muted the notifications.

Nothing, though.

She was busy. Or offended.

Maybe he should call her.

Well, that was reckless. But what did he have to lose here? He might have a nice conversation with an interesting woman, or she might not be interested, and he would never see her again.

Either way, he was likely to never see her again.

As he finished the last succulent morsel of salmon, the phone chimed with a text.

Calie.

Put away the manual and watch a movie.

. . .

He texted back,

I am watching a movie. Fargo. What manual?

You're such a bad liar.

I never lie.

Another lie!

He was caught out, of course. But there was little enough time at work to go through the manuals, and it was more relaxed at home anyway. And he never overwhelmed himself by trying to read dozens of pages. Two or three was fine.

Did you hear from her? Calie texted.

Brent put the phone aside and took his plate to the sink. He rinsed the things and ran through the regular tidying up rituals. He had a drawer dishwasher, which was plenty for a single man living alone, and he loaded the plate and utensils.

There were still dishes in it from the night when Alicia

had stayed over. When they'd had pizza and the cooked breakfast.

They'd sat around the table with the bacon and eggs.

Right here at his table.

He looked at it now, with his phone lying there face down. Waiting for a text back from her.

He was turning into a basket case, right here in his own kitchen.

Putting a tab in the dishwasher's receptacle, he closed the machine up and started the cycle. The sink pipe gurgled and the dishwasher hummed away merrily to itself.

His phone chimed again, and that little dopamine dripper in his brain gave him a tingle.

Most likely it was Calie again. Encouraging him to reply.

Brent dried his hands and checked the phone.

It was Red.

Good work on the reports there. Turns out there will be a whole bunch more.

Brent's heart sank.

The phone chimed again.

But it's all on me, Red texted. *Leave it in my hands.*

. . .

Then again.

Take a couple of days. I'm serious.

Brent tapped in,

I can't leave it all to you.

He sent it, and a moment later the phone rang. Red.

"Hi," Brent said.

"Easier to talk than texting," Red said. "I'm all thumbs on this thing anyway."

"You're supposed to be all thumbs."

"You know what I mean. So, I'm going to book you my friend's cabin up at Cloudhead Lake. Shane already told me it's empty. He's down in Anchorage wheeling and dealing as he does. Do you know the place?"

"I do. You and Shane took me and Calie one other time. Did Calie put you up to that?"

Cloudhead Lake was a gorgeous, small body of water surrounded by steep hills, and not more than fifteen miles from Candleton.

"Calie?"

"She's been matchmaking me with this woman from the flight. She's up in Candleton now."

"Huh. How about that? And while Calie didn't put me up to it, she did ask me about the cabin earlier today. Actually when I mentioned that I might have to furlough you."

"I'm being furloughed?"

"On full pay! Just until we get this license thing sorted. And if I do the furlough thing, you're not using your vacation days."

"I don't mind using my vacation days."

"I do! It seems hardly fair that you've got to take vacation because of some clerical error down in Anchorage."

"You're a good boss, Red."

"I know that. Now, listen. Do you want the cabin? It's empty for a full week right now. I can leave the keys in my mailbox and you can get started before first light, if you like."

"Tempting."

"Better than tempting. Obligatory."

Brent laughed. "All right. You talked me into it."

"Good. And put away the manual already, for goodness sakes. Relax man."

Another laugh. "Okay. I'll put away the manual. I'll pack and watch a movie and I'll be on the road before sunup."

"Attaboy."

Chapter Twenty-Eight

Alicia stared at her phone.

Brent had sent a text almost hour ago. Just on sunset.

I'd like to see that.

Meaning he'd like to see her being reckless. Why did that just make her tingle? And tingle all over?

It was excitement. Anticipation.

And she should be focusing on getting the house taken care off. Tidying up after the delicious grinder-hero-hoagie-sub thing she'd eaten. Full of fresh vegetables and perfect cuts of shaved ham.

And extraordinary too. Somewhere in her misguided, biased brain, she'd imagined Alaska as being home to restaurants that served only salmon or crab or venison steak. Of course it was just like anywhere. After all, Oklahoma had more than just cornbread, okra and onion burgers.

Still, it was a different world out here. The sun. The mountains. The air.

The bureaucracy.

Alicia tried to put that out of her head, and she showered and got ready for bed. She sat on the corner of the spare bed ruffling a towel through her hair, while David showered. The water hissed and the vapor wended its way through the upper floor.

After a relaxing meal and half of a dumb rom-com movie, they'd agreed to call it quits and pick up with the house sorting in the morning.

David was fine with sleeping in their father's bed. They'd stripped it and run the sheets through the laundry. Very practical.

Alicia draped the towel over the door handle, ready to hang when the bathroom was clear. She checked her phone.

A late text from Olivia.

And a text from Brent.

Alicia desperately wanted to read it, but she just went to the one from Olivia. Probably some drama and Alicia needed to just get that out of the way.

Sure enough, Olivia was dealing with some letter from the school. One of the kids, Linden, had been misbehaving. She'd fought with another kid and damaged a textbook. It wasn't the first time. Things were getting worse. Olivia had tried everything.

They'd been over it before. Alicia gave what little advice she could, but since she didn't yet have kids of her own, she always felt like she was coming at it from a wildly uninformed position. And Olivia had Greg. The marriage was solid, and they could talk about most everything.

Still, sometimes Olivia did need just to vent, really. Needed a friend who wasn't a parent.

Send Linden to me in Alaska, Alicia texted back, hoping the humor wasn't lost. *I'll sort her out.*

She waited a moment, but there was no response. It was after midnight in Tulsa, though, so if Olivia had any sense, her phone was off.

Alicia felt for her, but things would work out.

She opened up the text from Brent.

I'm coming up to a cabin at Cloudhead Lake near Candleton, he'd texted. *If you need a break, the scenery is awesome and the fish are amazing.*

A little charge went through her.

Another text came in right then.

Sorry, got that out of order. How are you? How are things going with the house and your brother?

. . .

She smiled. Out of order, but actually a better order.

An invitation to go to a lake with amazing scenery and awesome fish. Sounded fabulous.

But she had things to get on with here. With not much time to get it all done.

She started typing.

Things are going

But she stopped. How were things going?

Better than she'd expected. Worse than she'd wanted. They were making progress on the house, but she hadn't been prepared for the emotional wrench of it all. She dealt with houses and property all the time, but at a distance. Those developments existed mostly on paper. It was rare that she ever got to actually see them. And if she did, she never saw them again. They would be a cluster of run down houses, or a field, or graded land pegged out, with some of the utility infrastructure already being dug in. A couple of times, she had seen the finished developments. Bungalows and villas sitting on manicured lawns, with sidewalks that were perfectly flat and trees that were held in place by stakes. SUVs already parked on unstained concrete driveways and fallen tricycles already lying on front yards.

And here she was now, living through the vaguely similar early stages of that. Farewelling her father as the city tried to hustle along removal and demolition to move in families.

. . .

Things are going swimmingly. Does the cabin have a bathroom?

She sent it. Suitably offhand, but also very practical.

Who knew what he was offering really anyway? He might just be talking into the wind. Whatever that actually meant.

Along the hallway, the shower shut off. The house fell suddenly quiet.

Oh the peace. Suburban Tulsa was never this quiet.

A text came in.

Chemical bathroom. Running water. Gas cooking. Solar power.

Then another.

Bring a swimsuit.

She smiled. A rustic cabin in the wilds, but she could swim. She texted back.

It's winter. Did you not notice the ice everywhere?

. . .

Almost right away his response came.

It's spring, but I understand how you could make that mistake.

She could even hear him laughing at that. Good. It was meant to be a joke, really. She knew the seasons well enough. But then, if this was spring, winter up here must be truly numbing. She was something like two thousand miles closer to the north pole than she was at home.

The cabin has a hot tub.

A little thrill ran through her. The idea of sitting with him in a hot tub was arousing. Out in whatever kind of wonderful isolated scenery was out there. Far from anyone else.

"Calm down girl," she whispered to herself.

The sound of the bathroom door jerked her back to where she was. Back to the practicality of why she was here in Alaska in the first place.

She sighed.

I'm not an expert, she texted, *but is solar power really enough to run a hot tub?*

.   .   .

Electricity, he texted back, *is not the only way to heat water.*

A fire then? The place was sounding better all the time. She started to type in her response, but then another text came in from him.

It's a one-person tub. There's a wetback in the cabin's fire. Also, enough wood to last through an actual winter.

Then a moment later,

Not that I expect to stay that long.

Alicia smiled.

David knocked on her door. She set her phone aside and opened the door.

"Hey," she said. David had a towel around his waist. There was a little gray in his chest hair, and a little more weight than there probably should be.

Alicia smiled to herself. Who was she to judge?

"Pancakes at seven?" he said. "I'm making."

"You bet. You're being very nice."

He glanced at the door to their father's bedroom. "I guess that being up here kind of levels things. It makes your mortality a little clearer." He looked at her again. "It makes you realize what's important and what's not."

His eyes were baleful and he opened his arms up to her.

"Ew!" she yelped. "I'm not hugging you when you're still all drippy and wearing just a towel."

Back on her bed, the phone chimed.

"You're getting a few texts there. I didn't know you were like that."

"Like what?"

"A phone-a-holic."

"That's a terrible word. Did you make that up just now?"

"No, I use it a lot." His brow creased a little.

"Please don't. Just stop using it. Don't say it to me. Don't say it to anyone else ever." She laughed.

"What? Really?"

"Yes. It's gone. Forget that it ever existed."

Her phone chimed again.

David looked at it. Then back at her.

"Are you blushing?" he said.

"I just had a shower. I'm still hot."

"You had a shower fifteen minutes ago. And this house is cold. You've had oodles of chance to cool down."

"Also 'oodles'. Remove that from your vocabulary."

"Done. Never saying that again." He took a step toward their father's bedroom. "And I also appoint you as my new vocabulary coach."

"Nope. That's too big of a job."

He laughed. "Goodnight, sister of mine. Don't stay up too late texting with that guy."

She felt her blush increasing, and David laughed again.

He vanished into the room and closed the door behind him.

Alicia tried not to dash to her phone, but she did. Grabbed it up.

Or I could just drop by Candleton while I'm staying in the area. Take you for coffee.

Or dinner?

It was uplifting. Being invited to a cabin with a hot tub. Asked out for dinner.

When both of them knew it would lead nowhere.

Or could it?

She texted back.

Dinner sounds nice. A good break. Then when you come out to OK, I can take you to a real restaurant.

She sent it before she changed her mind.

Would that put him off? Was she being too forward?

Well, he was the one who'd invited her to a cabin with a hot tub.

Still, even if none of this went anywhere, it was nice just feeling some connection. Connection without any baggage.

She smiled to herself. Thinking *if none of this went anywhere*. Of course it was not going anywhere. So why not have some fun?

Her phone chimed again.

Tomorrow night? Pick you up around seven?

Alicia had to smile. That was just so very ordinary. So very wonderful.

She texted back,

See you then.

And, steeling herself, she switched her phone to silent and put it on the bedside table.

After her day, she would sleep well. Even if there were distracting, niggling, delicious thoughts of that fire fighter who was going to take her out to dinner tomorrow.

But distracting thoughts were good.

Very good.

Chapter Twenty-Nine

With the low, sharp rays of a brilliant morning sun lighting his house, Brent stumbled to the shower and let the pressure massage his back.

Should have a cold shower, really. After last night.

After texting Alicia so much.

Asking her up to the cabin with him. Asking her for dinner.

Almost as if some little alien creature had taken control of his brain for a moment. Like an excited kid racing in for some new, anticipated experience, without any regard.

All the while, he'd been able to hear Calie's voice in the back of his head. Asking him what he had to lose. Telling him he might as well have a little fun. Especially on his days off.

And he had days off. How about that?

It had a been a while. There were plenty of rostered days away from work, of course, but he either just stuck around

home—and read manuals if he was honest—or he had something planned. A fishing trip, or getting right out of town, like
that concert in Seattle.

He shut off the shower. Dried and dressed in jeans, boots,
tee shirt and a jacket. Grabbed a bowl of cereal for breakfast.
He tossed some gear in a couple of bags. His sister Jay would
call it a poor excuse for packing. She would have lists and be
scouring online forums for hints on how to be efficient with
space and gear.

The one time she'd visited, deep into fall, she'd brought
only a carry-on bag. But she'd made it work. She'd worn a
long, thick coat on the plane and in her bag she had micro-
thermal this and heat-retaining that. Expensive gear that he'd
figured she would likely never ever need back in the heat of
Albuquerque.

She had reminded him that the city was more than a mile
high, so winters definitely got cold.

"Not Alaska-cold," she'd said, "but nothing I've brought
along here is going to waste."

Brent tossed some beers and actual food into a cooler and
hauled the bags and the cooler out to the truck and got on the
road. He stopped at Annie's coffee cart for a brew. A venti.

Before lunch, he'd bumped and bumbled the pickup up
over the rough road to the cabin. In places, the tree-lined
road had been deeply rutted and he was glad of the pickup's
four wheel drive.

He'd parked up and gotten inside.

The inside air was stale, but the interior was just perfect.
Rustic and compact. Wooden floors and walls. Exposed beams

on the ceiling. The bedroom was separated by a simple curtain from the main room, and a bay window that looked out across the gorgeous, glistening inky surface of Cloudhead Lake.

Brent got the firebox going and checked that the water was flowing. Checked that the little battery had some power stored, and made sure that the solar circuit was working.

The first time he'd come up, Red hadn't mentioned the power thing, and Brent had spent the night in the dark, unable to charge his phone. The owner, Red's friend, had given Red the set of instructions, but Red had failed to pass them on.

Still, it hadn't mattered so much. There was a stack of firewood about as big as the cabin itself, and the whole idea of the place was getting away from things. Already Brent felt his shoulders relaxing and time just drifting.

He sat on the comfy squab in the bay window reading a Grisham paperback he'd brought along. He made a sandwich for lunch.

He kept the fire stoked.

Some time he ought to come out here for a week and just shut off. Completely shut off. The place was just idyllic.

The thick forest of ash and pines rustled in the light winds. Ripples formed on the lake as fish jumped. High, scudding clouds crossed the sky. A wading bird strode along near the cabin, head tipping back and forth as it looked for its next meal. Other birds called from their perches, hidden away in the trees.

Around six, Brent wondered where the afternoon had

gone, but was glad of it. Whiling away the time on nothing. It wasn't like him. It had to be healthy and restorative.

But it did mean it was time to head for Candleton and his date.

A date.

Crazy. Going out for a meal with a woman from Oklahoma. A wonderful, remarkable woman who'd walked into his life and was about to walk out again, with the precision of a surgeon removing a heart.

He dressed in his best jeans and a dark blue button shirt. Threw on a sport jacket. He stood by the pickup a moment, just savoring the air.

It would have been nice to have spent time with her out here, but he was fantasizing of course. Even a date was pretty amazing. Something to savor and look forward to.

About a mile from the cabin, still a couple of miles from paved road, the pickup's back tires went out, sliding to the left. Brent caught the slide easily, and slowed to let it diminish. As the back end came around, though, the front left wheel caught in one of the deeper ruts.

The truck jerked.

Brent steered with it.

Kept his feet off the pedals.

But the back end went around the wrong way. Around to the left.

The front wheel jammed in.

The running gear made a terrible sound.

Snapping and grinding.

The truck tipped. The rough road's angle was wrong. And the truck's weight shifted.

Through the steering wheel, Brent felt the chassis breaking.

The truck kept tipping.

With a terrible shattering sound, the truck slammed onto its left side.

The airbags blasted out at him. Smacked his head back.

The pickup slid along. Bumped up against a tree.

Brent lay on his side. Against the door's interior panel.

Dazed.

His head was against wet grassy ground. His right leg was jammed up against the steering column. His left leg might have been straight. He couldn't see it.

The knee hurt. Banged up on impact.

Where was his phone?

Automatically he felt his right back pocket, but it wasn't there. Of course. He didn't drive sitting on his phone. He'd left it in the drink holder in the central console.

Could be anywhere.

But when he looked, the phone was lying there. Kind of balanced on the edge. When he reached, though, his fingers shook and he bumped the phone. It fell. It landed on his thigh. Bounced and fell into the footwell.

Out of reach.

Chapter Thirty

Alicia couldn't believe how nervous she felt. Like when she'd been a teenager preparing for the prom.

How could she like this guy so much?

She'd been on plenty of other dates and they were like the old box of chocolates story. Some were fabulous and some were so-so and some were just better forgotten. Dates that should have stayed right there in the box.

She was actually in the bathroom applying makeup. Something she'd gone without for the last couple of days. After all, she was just tidying her father's house. After surviving an aircraft emergency.

She smiled to herself in the mirror. She stroked on a little mascara. Smacked her lips together and dabbed at the lipstick. Nothing too much. Just subtle. Brent seemed like a guy who wouldn't be fussed about makeup at all.

It was almost seven, and he didn't seem like a guy who would be late either.

In the mirror she did a final check, and headed out. She was wearing fitting Levi's and a nice pale blue blouse, with a pair of LeMaré low-heeled black pumps. When she came downstairs, David was in the living room, reclining on the sofa, phone in hand.

The fireplace was ablaze with glittering logs, giving the room a nice homey warmth.

"Well look at you," David said when she came in. "To the nines, huh?"

She laughed. "Dressed to the nines I would be in a slinky black dress, with my hair styled and so made up that I couldn't move my face."

"Well, I think you look like you're about to wow the guy."

That made her grin.

"Of course, he's already 'wowed', right?" David said. "Driving up here to see you."

"Distance is nothing in Alaska. Remember that?"

David gave a shake of his head. "Don't believe it. No guy drives three hours by mistake. You watch yourself, you'll wind up smitten and selling up your Tulsa place to move up here. Buy yourself a snow machine and a salmon farm."

"Funny." She held up her hands and counted off on her fingers. "One, I'm flattered, so that's nice. Two, did you notice the cold? It's a whole other order of cold to where we come from. I saw penguins walking down the street before."

"Penguins aren't in Alaska. Southern hemisphere only."

"Three, that was a joke. Four, I have a pretty nice life right there in Tulsa."

"Yes you do. Also, you need to work on your jokes."

"That's what I was doing. Working on it. In preparation for my date. I want to be funny and charming." She went and sat on the sofa next to him.

"Nervous huh?" David said.

"Why? Why would I be this nervous? I'm a grown woman."

"How long since you've had a date?"

"That's none of your business."

"That long huh?"

Alicia sighed, a little deflated.

"What?" David said.

"Finally I meet a guy who's nice and polite and..."

"A muscular fire-fighter?"

"Yes. All of that."

"A fabulous package."

"Stop it."

"He could be your soul mate, but he lives in Alaska, so how would that work? At least he's not gay."

"That would make it so much easier!"

David laughed.

"I'm a mess," she said. "You're right. I am smitten. He's so cute. I mean, soooo cute. And interesting and helpful and smart and polite and did I mention cute and I've only known him all of a few days and the first time we made eye contact was right when I'd come off the plane with engine trouble and–"

"Take a breath, sis. You're going to pass out."

"—it was like electricity."

Alicia stopped and took a breath and giggled. How come she was feeling comfortable around David all of a sudden? Usually talking like that was reserved for coffee with Olivia and Melissa.

Well, right now there was no one else. And she and David were siblings, after all.

Perhaps the loss of their father was drawing them closer. Especially since they'd had to travel such a long way to come here to sort things out.

"Thanks for coming up," she said. "It's good having you around."

"I know it. It's good hanging out with you too."

"When's he coming, then?"

"Seven."

David glanced at his phone. A video was playing there. A cat leaping onto a curtain and climbing to the lintel.

"Looks as if you have your evening taken care of," Alicia said.

"Jake sent it to me. He loves these things. From what I see, the internet was basically invented so we can laugh at house cats more."

"Yep. Wait, it's quarter after?" She leaned forward, looking at the tiny time in the corner of his phone screen.

"Quarter after seven," David said. "He must be just about here."

Alicia couldn't help herself. She stood and went to the

curtains. She opened a little gap and peered out into the chilly night.

Brent's pickup wasn't there.

"Probably just held up," David said.

"Probably." It didn't seem like Brent to be late. Maybe she was getting stood up.

Maybe there had been a wreck on the road and he was stuck behind it. Or was just helping out. Which would explain why he hadn't texted or called.

But still, it felt awkward. *She* felt awkward.

"Don't worry," David said.

"I'm not." She tried to sound casual. Tried not show how worried she was growing.

Already she was feeling emotionally wrung out from her father's death.

She didn't need this too.

Chapter Thirty-One

In the fallen pickup, Brent scrabbled around for his phone. He was jammed up in his seatbelt. The airbags had deflated, but his arm had gotten tangled and he'd had to extract it.

It was growing dark.

Had he bumped his head? Had he passed out?

He'd definitely lost time here. It had been around six when he'd set out. A long time from dusk.

The driver's window was gone. Shattered when the pickup had landed on its side.

Possibly from his head.

He couldn't remember the window shattering. Couldn't remember hitting his head. Perhaps those were good indications that he had taken a hit.

His head didn't feel hurt. He checked his scalp again for bleeding. Didn't feel any stickiness, nor any wound.

But he did find a lump. On the left, near the back of his head. It was tender to the touch.

As an emergency responder, it was his job to know all the things to do, but he was feeling dazed. Stunned.

Never before had he been in a wreck. Which was saying something out here. The way some people drove, and the treachery of some of the roads.

This one, for example.

He should have known better. Should have driven better.

Distracted, that's what it was. Anticipating his date with the wonderful Alicia, and forgetting to pay as much attention as he should.

He drove these kinds of roads plenty. Knew how to take it easy. He had a vehicle that was more than capable of negotiating rugged back blocks trails. This wasn't even the most challenging he'd ever been along.

Taking a breath, he leaned back against the seat. Through the windshield, he saw a shadowy shape moving at the edge of the trees. Perhaps an small elk. A juvenile. It darted away.

He was an awful long way from anywhere. And no one was expecting him for a couple of days.

Brent swore softly.

With his thumb, he tried to release the seatbelt again. The lock was jammed. He just couldn't get enough force on it to get the lock to release. The inertia reel mechanism had locked up and he couldn't get any stretch from the belt at all.

At least it wasn't so tight that he couldn't breathe.

If he had a blade, he could cut it. Get himself at least partly extracted.

He pushed up from the cold ground and stretched for the glove compartment. He had an old Leatherman multitool in there. For a while he'd worn it on his belt, but he'd kept catching the tool's sheath on things. Besides, he'd used it far less than he'd expected or intended. It was a handy thing to keep in the glove compartment.

Getting his fingers—just—on the glove compartment's latch, he scrabbled around. But he couldn't get a good grip.

He lay back against the door and the ground. What he needed was a lever or something to get at the latch.

Rooting around in the central console compartment, he found some gum and some change and a pin from the last Woodchuck Festival in Wilkes Landing. None of which were any use for opening the glove compartment.

But he had his keys still in his pocket.

It took some effort, given his jammed-up, hips-bent angle, but he managed to extract them. Stretching up again, he used his house key to flick open the glove compartment latch. His registration and insurance papers fell out, but nothing else.

The Leatherman had to be lying there, against the side.

Pulling on the gearstick, Brent stretched up as much as he could. His tendons complained and stung.

He still couldn't reach the tool.

Breathing hard now, he let himself lie and rest for a moment.

Didn't they tell people to take it easy? Even if you weren't hurt physically, you'd still been through a trauma and you needed time to recover.

Taking a breath, he scrabbled around some more. His left

knee hurt. He stretched and twisted, the belt holding him in place.

Straining, he got his fingers on the phone. It was right down at the bottom of the door. He moved slowly and gently. It wouldn't do to simply push it farther out of reach.

Painstakingly, he slid his fingers along the phone's edge.

He pushed. Twisted. Moved the phone a little.

Lifting his hand, he shifted his fingers. Placed them again.

Moved the phone another fraction.

He was breathing hard. The air was cool. He could smell the stink of fuel.

Hopefully that wouldn't come to anything.

In back was a little fire extinguisher. But it was out of reach.

He needed to get out of the truck. Away from it.

Needed to call for help.

He got a grip on the phone.

Slid it up.

The screen was blank.

A spiderweb of cracks ran across the display.

Chapter Thirty-Two

Alicia checked her phone again. No messages.

It would be fine. It would just be a simple thing. Brent had stopped to help someone change a tire or something. Just the kind of thing he would do.

Though wouldn't he text her? To let her know that he'd been held up.

She stood from the sofa and went to the fire. She held her hands out, enjoying the tingling warmth. Picking up the poker, she stirred the embers a little. She got a log and added it to the blaze.

"He's not going to stand you up," David said, still on the sofa with his phone.

"I know that. Because if he did, he would have to answer to you, right?"

"You bet. I'd show that muscular Alaskan fire-fighter a thing or two."

"You would." It was nice joking around, but there was a little cold stone growing in Alicia's belly. Worry. That fear of just not knowing.

"I'm going to make hot chocolates," David said. "Take your mind of it all."

"That's nice, thanks." She followed him to the kitchen, keeping her ear out for a knock at the door.

While David worked on making the hot chocolates, Alicia checked her phone.

No text. No messages.

Of course. It hadn't chimed at her. It wasn't as if it was suddenly going to quit with the notifications.

It was after twenty past seven.

From along the road came the slightly disturbing sounds of machinery. It was after whatever passed for rush hour in Candleton, and the crew were preparing to drive away that neighboring house.

Alicia rolled her shoulders.

"Worrying too much," David said. The electric kettle rumbled and steamed merrily.

"I just feel so... I don't know. Let down? You know, you build up your hopes and expectations and then reality comes rushing in."

Why was she feeling like this? It was nice to have the attention, but she had a life elsewhere. Thousands of miles away. Where it was actually warm most of the year.

The kettle clicked off and David poured the hot water over the cocoa mix. The smell was invigorating.

"The reality is," David said, "that you don't know. Until you do, you can't take it personally."

"I know. But that doesn't mean that my poor fragile heart actually understands that."

"Poor fragile heart?"

"It was an expression."

"You don't have fragile heart. You have more resilience than anyone I know. Francine included."

"Really?" David's wife Francine was one of the strongest people Alicia knew. Smart and capable. She would have done great in the realm of property development, where there were so many promises and so many grand ideas and, too often, a huge lack of follow-through.

"Really," David said. "And I know this is an emotional time. For both of us. I can't imagine what it's like for you adding in that hunk from the November page of the 'Fire-Fighters of Alaska' calendar."

"Hey!" But she was smiling. David could be quite disarming.

They took their hot chocolates back to the warmth of the living room and sat. Alicia watched the fire.

Then it was seven thirty.

"I think you can text," David said. "To check on his whereabouts. That's fair. A half hour late. See what kind of half-baked excuse he comes up with."

"Yep," she said, and texted. It took a couple of goes to get the words right.

.   .   .

Did we say seven for dinner?

That sounded right. She sent it.

There was no response.

She sipped at her hot chocolate. Paced a little. David kept watching cat videos.

Then it was seven forty-five.

Did I get the time wrong? Maybe the day?

She included a goofy smiley face emoji.

At eight, he still hadn't replied.

Alicia's mouth was dry. She'd been stood up a couple of times before, but usually she'd had a feeling that the guy was a jerk beforehand anyway.

No loss.

And even though in her head she knew this thing with Brent wouldn't go anywhere, it was clearly one of those times where her head and her heart were not communicating well.

Because there was this longing within her just to spend more time with him.

"Basket case," she whispered.

"What's that?" David said.

"Nothing." She took a breath. "I just need to get my head straight. Stop waiting around and use this time to get some sorting done."

"Alicia, come on. Relax for the evening, at least."

But she couldn't. She went up to the junk room and got one of the hefty old corrugated cardboard boxes of stuff and brought it back down to the living room.

She set the box on the coffee table and opened the flaps.

"Books," David said. "Books, books and more books."

Alicia got one out. It was a history of Alaska. From the nineteen seventies. It smelled musty and dated. She flicked through it.

There were notes in the margins. And scraps of paper fell out. Covered in their father's handwriting.

"Huh," David said, picking up one of the scraps. "That's something. Amateur historian."

"Who'd have thought?" Alicia sat down with the book.

At least it was something to take her mind off Brent. A little.

In fact, barely at all.

Chapter Thirty-Three

T he fire crackled and the warmth was invigorating. In their father's living room, David worked through the box of books. Alaska, Russia, Canada. Fisheries and logging and mining. Colonization and indigenous tragedies. Books from various viewpoints.

There were notebooks too, with scrawlings and diagrams on various pages.

"As if he was planning on putting together a book himself," David said.

"These were all just in a box," Alicia said. "It wasn't an active project."

She wasn't able to concentrate anyway. The books were a little distraction, but she found herself checking her phone.

"Now I'm really getting worried," Alicia said, staring at the blank space where Brent's text should have been.

"It'll just be a thing," David said. "Some emergency that he can't leave. And he isn't getting a chance to make contact. I mean, if you're going to hook up with an emergency responder, this is part of the package."

"It's not a package. It's dinner."

"Tell yourself that. I saw your eyes. I see how you are now."

She looked away. The fire was dying down. She stood and added in another log. As much for something practical to do as for the warmth.

David had put down the book he'd been flicking through. He sipped from his own hot chocolate. It was good having him around.

She smiled at herself. That was a surprise.

Eight oh five.

Instead of texting, Alicia called Brent's number. She got his missed call message. It was nice to hear his voice, at least.

"Hey," she said after the tone, "I hope everything's all right. I guess you're off on some emergency. Let me know how things are."

She ended the call and stared at the phone for a moment.

"Good," David said. "It'll be fine. And I think we were ambitious to imagine that we could tidy Dad's place in a couple of days. It's going to take longer than we might have hoped. We'll be around for a while." He lifted another of the books from the box. Denali National Park.

"Assuming," Alicia said, "they don't load us onto a truck and haul us up to Teakball for a mining house."

"Assuming."

Alicia sat again and found the number for the Wilkes Landing airport. She called.

Got a recorded message.

With a little more digging, she found the number for the Wilkes Landing city council. The phone was answered by Leili, a chirpy woman who told Alicia that there were no current emergencies that were showing up on her list.

"But it's after hours here," Leili said. "So let me put you on hold and check with the police and the hospital. It should all show up on my board here."

"Please," Alicia said. "I'm worried."

"Oh, I can understand that. I'll be right back with you."

The phone clicked and the sound of an instrumental lounge version of Coldplay's song *Yellow* piped through. That made Alicia think of Brent and their kind of matching tee shirts, and then of Brent out of his tee shirt. With those defined muscles and that dark curly hair.

She was definitely becoming a basket case.

Who'd have thought that all this would spark something within her?

"I'm back!" Leili said from the phone. "Are you still there?"

"Yes."

"Hey, there's nothing going on. I can't say why you can't reach him. I called there too, but his phone's just going to message. I guess it's just switched off. Maybe he's catching up on sleep?"

"Maybe. Are you able to give me Calie's number?" Alicia realized that she didn't know Calie's full name.

"I can't give out numbers. My apologies."

"No of course. Sorry, I shouldn't have asked." Alicia felt so isolated right then. "How about this, though. I'm a kind of a new friend, and I was expecting Brent to show up here. Could you perhaps get a message to Calie and ask her to call me? Alicia Brooks."

"That, I can do. I have your number right here on my screen. And message sent."

"Oh, thanks, Leili. You're a gem."

"Thank you! Was there anything else I can help with?"

"Not right now, thanks."

"You have a good evening. I hope this all works out for you. Bye now."

"Bye." Alicia tapped to end the call.

Almost right away her phone rang, startling her.

An unknown number.

She answered.

"Alicia?" Calie. "I got a message that you're trying to reach me, because you can't reach Brent?"

"I feel silly now," Alicia said. "Just that we were going on a... date, but he hasn't shown up. I probably shouldn't worry, but his phone's not..." She sighed. "I guess he just got busy."

"Nope. Brent doesn't 'just get busy'. Not when he's got a date with a certified babe."

Alicia felt herself blushing. She was no babe, but from Calie it sounded sweet.

"Can you reach him?" Alicia said.

"Same way as you, by phone. But I'll go around to his place to check. Right now. I'll be giving him a quick kick up the butt if he's there."

"He said he was going to a cabin? Up this way somewhere."

"A cabin?"

"He invited me up. Said that he was there for a couple of days. Tempted as I was, I still have Dad's estate to work through." Somehow she was sounding calmer than she felt.

"Right," Calie said. "Red kicked Brent out for a couple of days. That'll be Shane Resston's place. He and Red are friends. I've been up there before. I think there's no cell coverage, but then, welcome to Alaska. Listen, let me make a couple of calls and come back to you."

"Okay."

"Don't worry. He'll be there. Or he'll have to answer to me."

"And my brother." Alicia's eyes flicked to David, watching her from the other sofa.

"Then you're covered. Talk soon."

Calie rang off.

Chapter Thirty-Four

Brent's phone powered up with a long touch.

The display flickered and jittered as the starting icons and welcomes appeared.

In theory the cabin was out of range of any cell tower—that was the appeal of the place—but perhaps there was some vague reception he could get.

If the phone would actually work.

He was feeling clearer-headed now. But with the clearing of he head had come the pain. Definitely a bad knock. A mild concussion. At least.

Idiot. He should have been driving more cautiously. Of course.

It was embarrassing, really. The first responder who tipped his truck over on a simple country road. They would find his mummified body in a few months and say nice things at the funeral, but they would all be thinking what a jerk he'd been. Should have known better.

The phone's icons appeared across the display. Ghosted and broken under the web of cracks in the glass.

He tapped the call icon.

Nothing happened.

He tried several more times. With his finger at different angles. Tried with his thumb and with different fingers.

He swiped from the top to bring down the menu, but that didn't work either.

The phone was shot.

He tried to tap into his contacts, to maybe call directly from there. But the contacts wouldn't come up either.

Holding the phone close and squinting, he could see that he had a single bar of connection. As he watched, it dropped to no bars. Then came back to one bar.

Somewhere in moving the phone around and brushing the screen, he inadvertently opened up the messages.

A series of them from Alicia.

See you then.

Did we say seven for dinner?

Did I get the time wrong? Maybe the day?

.   .   .

The last two had just been sent an hour or so ago.

He needed help here, though. He needed to contact emergency services.

But the phone was busted. He didn't even dare go back to the list and text Calie.

If the phone would even work to just contact Alicia.

Not daring to hope, he tapped to reply.

The blank space came up, with the little flashing cursor. And the thumb keyboard.

He started tapping in.

Had a wreck. Send help.

He stared at the words. Too bald. Too bland.

Not specific enough.

The phone's display flickered. He couldn't trust it.

He added two words.

Near cabin

And he still didn't dare hope.

The connection switched from one bar to none.

Back to one.

He tapped to send the text.

A tiny dotted spinning dial came up. He'd never even seen it before. Texts just went instantly.

It was as if the phone was thinking about it.

One bar. No bars.

One bar again.

He held the phone up a little.

The dial vanished.

And the time came up.

The time that the text had gone through.

"Please," he whispered, feeling himself growing light-headed again.

Chapter Thirty-Five

L eaning back in her father's old sofa Alicia paced in her head. Back and forth. Eyes closed.

The fire crackled. David was quietly sorting the books.

"Dad needed a computer," David said. "Instead of making scrappy notes and writing in the margins of books. I've got a friend who's a librarian would be just horrified by the vandalism. With a computer Dad could have kept everything in order."

"Perhaps Dad wasn't working on a project that needed any order." Alicia kept her eyes closed. "Perhaps he was just having fun."

"Yeah maybe."

Alicia's phone rang with an incoming call. As she picked it up, it chimed for a text too.

The call was the same unknown number. Calie.

"Hello?" Alicia said. "Calie."

"Brent's not at his place. His truck is gone. I called Red who said that Brent definitely took the keys to Shane's cabin."

"Maybe Brent got a flat tire," Alicia said. "Just out of cell phone range."

"Could be. But look, I'm driving up there. I'm already in my truck and putting the phone into the hands-free bracket."

"Do you have to go up there?"

"Yes."

"Isn't it a long way?"

"Couple of hours. Closer to you actually."

"Send me directions."

"Nah, you don't want to go messing with that. What kind of car have you got?"

"I don't. David's got a... what is your rental David? A Prius or something?"

"A Prius," Calie said. "It's a four wheel drive road. And for experienced drivers. You don't want to put a little family car on that. The thing would have a nervous breakdown."

"It's an SUV," David said. "A Subaru. I'm not coming to Alaska and renting a Prius."

"Not that we have anything against a Prius," Alicia said, putting her phone on speaker.

"You should," Calie said. "What did he say? A Subaru?"

"Yes," David said. "It has new-car smell. Less than fifteen hundred miles on the clock."

"Hmm. That sounds nice."

"So I'll go," Alicia said, standing. "Tell me the directions."

"Alicia. It's best if you sit tight." From the background came the sounds of Calie's vehicle. Engine. Tires on the road.

"You said he's closer to me," Alicia said. "So I can get to him more quickly."

"Just leave it with me," Calie said. "It's probably nothing. We're probably over-reacting. I'll get up there and he'll look at me like I'm a doofus, then I'll remind him that he stood you up, and then who's the doofus?"

"You're not over-reacting," Alicia said. "Something's not right. I can sense it."

Calie took a beat, then said, "Yes, I sense it too."

"What are we sensing here?" David said.

"Brent wouldn't stand someone up," Calie said.

"Something's happened," Alicia said. The fire crackled, but a chill ran through her. Now she was pacing with her feet, rather than just in her head.

"Sit tight," Calie said.

She sat again. "All right. It goes against my better instincts."

Wait, a text had come in.

She tapped her phone and brought it up.

"I'll call soon," Calie said. "Once I know something. Stay by the phone. I'll keep in touch with updates."

The text came up.

From Brent.

Had a wreck. Send help. Near Cabin.

. . .

The world seemed to stop. It froze into a single solid block. Every nerve in Alicia's body tingled.

"Bye now," Calie said.

"Wait," Alicia said. "I just—"

But Calie had gone.

Alicia tapped to call her back, but at the same time, she looked over at David.

"What?" David said.

"I need your keys."

Chapter Thirty-Six

David insisted on driving.

"Look at you," he said. "You're nervous as anything. Worried. And you need to navigate. And call Calie. And text Brent."

Alicia had already texted Brent back, telling him they were on their way, but there was still no response.

"I know," she said. "But I'll feel better behind the wheel. Like I'm in action." It felt like David was shutting her down.

They stood at the curb, outside their father's house. The air was so cold it made he breath come out in plumes.

Brent had had a wreck. What did that mean?

She had to get up there.

"Get in," David said, opening the Subaru's passenger door. "Let me drive."

"Stop it. And I have a one word answer which trumps everything else."

"Which is?"

"Insurance."

"Oh, right." He would have the rental company's standard package, but it wouldn't have included her as a driver. If she, nervous as she was, even scraped the paintwork, it would just be compounding things.

"So get in," David said.

In moments they were underway. Alicia didn't even know exactly where they were going. David cranked up the car's heat as she called up the maps on her phone. The new car smell was strong.

"Where are we headed?" he said.

"Out of town. Lake Cloudtop. South. Take a left up here. That'll get you toward the highway to Wilkes Landing."

Assuming that was the right way to go.

Cones of mist hung around the streetlights. There was no one out and about.

Alicia scrolled back through Brent's texts. *Cloudhead Lake*, not Lake Cloudtop.

Zooming out on the map, from Candleton, she tapped in for a search. She put in the name.

It didn't come up.

She cursed.

"What?" David said.

"Can't find it." She tapped the phone to call Calie. David had been right. It was better with him driving.

Calie answered right on the first ring.

"Alicia?" she said. "I don't have any updates."

"We're on the road," Alicia said.

"Ah, girl, you shouldn't be. Stay warm and safe."

"I got a text from him. 'Had a wreck. Send help. Near Cabin.'."

Calie swore.

"Why did he text me?" Alicia said. "Why not call you? Or emergency services?"

"Let's figure that out later. The turn to Cloudhead Lake must be about twenty, twenty-one miles from Candleton."

"Okay. I can't find it on the maps."

"Yeah, maybe it's too little. The road should be there. I can't remember the name. Try Resston. With two esses. Their family owns a big block of land there."

Alicia put the name in. The map swirled around and showed her Resston Road.

"Got it," she said, and tapped to turn on the GPS.

The map swirled some more and a soft female voice said, "In five hundred yards, turn left."

"I can do that," David said.

"We're en-route," Alicia said.

"Good," Calie said. "Stay in touch."

Alicia ended the call.

Then they were out of town, leaving the streetlights and homes behind. None of it seemed very important right now. Not sorting out their father's things. Not the orders from the city.

Brent had been in a wreck.

What about the other people? Had a truck swiped him from the highway? Was he lying upside down in a river?

Surely the other driver would have stopped to help.

Leili had said there were no emergencies.

When had Brent's text come in? It was after she'd spoken to Leili. Perhaps there were emergency services on the way already.

Alicia crossed her arms and put her hands up on her shoulders. She dug her fingers in, massaging at muscles and tendons.

She was overthinking it.

"In five hundred yards," the soft GPS voice said, "bear right and follow Kelly Avenue into Morgan Road."

"Got it," David said.

Tapping her phone, Alicia called Calie again.

"Here," Calie said.

"Shouldn't we call emergency services?" she said.

"Did you get another text from him?"

"No." Alicia checked again. No more texts.

"Okay. So I've already called SAR, but we don't have a location."

"SAR?"

"Search and rescue."

"Okay. They have a helicopter, right?"

"That's what they have, yes."

"Should they not be on their way?"

"If they knew where to go."

"Cloudhead Lake. Is that as hard for them to find as it was for me?"

"Nope. But they need to know more. Something precise."

"Can they not get the location from his cellphone. You know, triangulating the signal or something?"

"They'll be working on it."

"Okay."

"They don't send the choppers up on a whim," Calie said. "That's why I'm going up there. To check."

"It'll take you too long."

Calie didn't respond.

"In seventeen miles," the GPS said, "take a right onto Resston Road."

The dark of the Alaskan night whipped by. Trees. The road's guard rail. The Subaru's headlights shone away across the slick tarmac.

Far ahead the red taillights of a truck shone back at them. The road had an upward grade. Pulling up through the hills that stood around Candleton.

Alicia had a moment of panic, imagining that it was the house that was getting hauled away, and that it would be impossible to get past it.

But they were taking the truck north. To Teakball.

Alicia glanced at the speedo. David was doing close to sixty. The road's posted limit. But it was dark. Probably icy.

How did people live up here?

"It's all we can do, right now," Calie said from the phone. "Brent knows what to do. If he was able to text you, then that's a good sign. A real good sign."

"I hope so. I really do."

"I know it. Don't worry. I'll call you back when I hear any updates."

"Thank you."

David eased back on the accelerator as they came up behind the truck.

"Going to be tricky to pass," he said.

It was just a semi. The big rectangle of the back doors shone back at them. *Trust Gilbert's* big letters said across the top. *On Time Deliveries. Every Time.*

The truck was moving somewhere under fifty.

"I'll find somewhere to pass," David said, easing out a little across the centerline.

"Don't wreck us too," Alicia said.

"No. You better believe that I'm being cautious."

Chapter Thirty-Seven

Brent shivered, lying against the cold ground and the truck's door. In almost complete darkness.

The seatbelt cut into him. He'd tried again to release the latch, but had gotten nowhere.

His phone had given up entirely. It didn't respond to the buttons. The cracked screen stayed blank.

Maybe the text had gone through.

He tried to keep himself curled up. Trying to conserve body heat.

In back he had all the gear he would need. Survival blanket. A little gas stove that he could have heated water on. Could have made himself a nice coffee.

Another knife he could have used to cut the seatbelt webbing. Flares. Gloves and socks and a scarf. He was just used to keeping all this stuff in the truck. Ready to go.

All of it out of reach now.

There was even an EPIRB emergency locator beacon. If he'd set it off, the responders would have run some checks, like calling his contacts, to make sure it hadn't been set off accidentally. Then they would have sent people to his location.

Probably in a helicopter.

He cursed. If he made it out of this, he was going to put a knife and the EPIRB in a satchel and keep it in the central console. Right there. Right within reach.

If he made it out of this! What kind of thinking was that?

Nope. He had to make it out of this.

Had to figure his way through.

If he could get out of the seatbelt, then he could work out anything else. He had the gear. An old phrase ran around his head. *Seatbelts save lives.* He knew it. In his time with various emergency outfits, he'd seen it numerous times.

And seen it when the lack of a seatbelt had cost a life.

It was the rare occasion when a seatbelt made things worse.

He tried the latch again. No dice.

Taking his keys, he slipped the truck's physical key out of the fob and felt along the edge. Kind of like a blunt serrated knife.

Feeling his way along the seatbelt strap, he found a spot near his right hip where he might actually get some purchase. Get the right angle to begin sawing back and forth.

It would probably take hours, if it could be done at all. With good reason, seatbelt webbing was ridiculously strong.

But then, it wasn't as if he had anywhere to be.

Except for his date.

With Alicia.

Over in Candleton.

Chances were, she was just plain annoyed with him for standing her up. That text had probably never even reached her.

Well, it had looked nice for a moment there.

He set to sawing, aware that by the time he actually managed to cut himself free, Alicia would be long gone. Back in Oklahoma, happily enjoying the sunshine and warmth.

The webbing made an odd sound as he worked the makeshift blade back and forth. Kind of like a ratchet. Like some musical band that worked exclusively with found instruments.

He kept at it. Counting as he went. He would check every fifty strokes. Just to see if he'd made any headway.

He wasn't so very hopeful.

Chapter Thirty-Eight

A licia watched the road through the Subaru's wash of headlights as David slowed for the turn to Resston Road. Another vehicle was coming toward them, headed up from Wilkes Landing.

Part of Alicia just wished that the occupant could be Calie. That she had broken every road rule and a few laws of physics just to race them to the scene of Brent's wreck.

"Turn here," the GPS said.

The other vehicle raced on by. David made the turn.

"Your destination," the GPS said with cheery neutrality, "is in twelve miles."

"Great," David said, peering ahead.

The road was gravel. Or dirt. It looked in pretty good shape.

A little niggle swam through the back of Alicia's head.

Something about a time when she'd rented a vehicle and the agent at the desk had mentioned that the insurance got nullified if she damaged the vehicle on an unpaved road and the damage was due to the road's condition.

Hardly mattered right now.

She checked her phone for texts from Brent.

Nothing.

She called Calie.

"Hey there," Calie said. She sounded tired.

"We're on Resston Road," Alicia said.

"Good. Take it easy. It's not your everyday dirt road. Go slower than you think you need to."

"Understood," David said.

Alicia glanced over. He was practically idling along at all of twenty miles an hour. The road rumbled under the tires. The wheel arches rattled with stones.

"Also," Calie said, "keep your eyes wide for him. If he's had a wreck, maybe he's gone off the road. You could miss him in the dark."

"I know it," Alicia said. "Are you far away?"

"Thirty, forty minutes."

That seemed like not so much.

"You remember to take it easy too," Alicia said. "You're no use to anyone if you crash too."

"Understood. And call me if—"

Alicia waited a moment for Calie to finish.

"Calie?"

But the call had ended. The phone's display showed no bars. One bar flicked. Vanished again.

"Out of coverage?" David said.

"Yes."

"GPS?"

"Still working." Alicia turned the phone face down. "Hardly matters. We're on the right road, as far as we know."

"He said 'near the cabin', didn't he?"

"Near the cabin."

The headlights cast eerie momentary glows through the trees, leaving deep shadows that vanished into dark.

The road wound back and forth, left and right. Long slow curves, followed by some tight turns. In places there was a stream running next to them. Mostly the stream was hidden in the trees.

The road narrowed as they progressed. If they met someone coming the other way, one of them would have to back up and find a spot wide enough for the other to get by.

The Subaru rocked back and forth in pits and hollows. Some were water-filled. Some formed longer ruts.

"Terrible road," David said.

"I can see that," Alicia said. "And feel it."

"I don't want to go any slower. Likewise, I don't want to wreck the car."

"No, it's fine. Don't go faster. This speed, it's easier to try to spot his truck."

"A cop car would have a spotlight."

"I know."

Alicia leaned forward. She scanned left and right. Trying to catch anything in the backwash of the headlights.

Very aware that each time they turned, the lights were

facing away from the inside of the turn. Could he have gone off in one of those?

Wouldn't it be more likely to crash on the outside of a bend?

How fast had he been going? Could he have bounced away through the trees? He could be just thirty yards from the road and be invisible. Hidden in the foliage.

Alicia's phone rang.

She answered.

"Calie?"

"So there's GPS data from his phone. I had to pull some strings to get it looked up, but I have it. It looks like he was a little more than three miles from the cabin. There's not current signal from the phone."

"A little more than three miles?" Alicia said. "We were twelve miles from it when we left the main road. More or less. I mean, I just put in where the road ended at the lake."

"That'll do it. So when you've gone nine miles, you should be right on him. If you've gone ten, turn around."

"Understood."

"Shoot," David said. "I didn't look at the odometer when we turned."

"You said, less than fifteen hundred miles on the clock right? When you picked it up?"

"Yes. Fourteen forty one. I remembered it because it was a palindrome. Excuse me being geeky on that."

"No, it's good. What's it reading now?" Already Alicia was working through the maps on her phone. It was going to be rough, but better than driving blind.

"Now it's fifteen oh-six."

"How far do you figure we've been on this road?"

"A few miles, maybe? Hard to say in the dark."

Alicia ran through the maps, charting out the Subaru's movements. From the airport to Bondurant Street. In to city hall and back. And then up to the turn onto Resston Road. Sixty-two miles.

"We've come around four miles," Alicia said. "So another five. Maybe." It felt like a vague, sloppy guesstimate.

"I've punched in the trip odometer," David said. "Set at zero now."

It was all very haphazard. Best-guesses and hope.

She focused back on the surroundings. The thickness of the trees. The dark shadows. The patches of light from the forest as lighter things shone the headlight glare back at them.

Something flashed by and she turned to watch it, heart in her throat.

Just a fencepost.

"Not it?" David said.

"Nope."

They drove on in silence.

Alicia's heart hammered at her. What if they'd gotten it all wrong? What if this wasn't the road at all?

What if she'd misunderstood Brent's text. What if it was all a big mistake?

It didn't seem likely.

She couldn't be here second-guessing all this.

Better to just get up here and take a look. Better to over-react than not react at all.

"Something up there?" David said, slowing.

It didn't feel like they'd come far enough. But then, that calculation could be well out.

She'd done it as much to occupy her mind as for anything else.

David was slowing, an Alicia saw what he'd seen.

A tractor. Parked alongside the road.

Old and rusting. Abandoned long ago.

"Nope," David said.

He accelerated a little. Edging along, really. Keeping the speed between fifteen and twenty.

The road really was rough. Rutted deeply in places. Almost impassable.

"Someone needs to come up here and do some work," David said. "If there's any money in Dad's estate, my first bill is going to be the repairs to this car."

"We'll split it," Alicia said. "In fact, I'll cover it. It's my fault we're up here."

"It's not your fault. It's that new boyfriend of yours. Crashing his car up here." David glanced over. "Probably because he was so distracted and excited about getting to go on a date with you."

"Wow. Both complimentary and insulting all at once."

"I'm well-practiced."

"I should know it."

Then she spotted something right at the edge of the head-lights. A gray shape.

The underside of a vehicle.
They'd almost gone right by.
"Stop!" she said. "Stop right here."

Chapter Thirty-Nine

T he air was bitingly cold when Alicia got out of David's rental Subaru. He was shouting at her. Something about waiting for him to come to a full stop.

But she was out and around the back of it.

The SUV bumped on.

The ground was slick. Muddy. The freezing air was surprisingly rich with the scent of it. And the smell of the trees.

She practically ran across to the fallen pickup. Almost invisible in the dark.

David was swinging the car around. It brought the head-lights to bear on the wreck.

Alicia saw how it had happened.

Skid marks through the mud. Brent had slid out. The tires

had caught on the hard edge of a rut. The truck had gone over.

From somewhere in the trees came the screech of a night bird.

Brent's pickup was lying on its driver's side. The back tire had blown out.

Alicia went around the hood. Wet grass grabbed at her legs.

The steel of the hood was cold as she used it to balance.

"Brent!" she called.

There was no response.

She crouched at the windscreen. Couldn't see inside. It was so dark.

Flicking on the flashlight on her phone, she shone the beam around.

Brent lay there. Against the door.

He was moving his arms. Rubbing something against the seatbelt.

He looked up at her, startled by the light.

"Alicia?" he said, his voice barely carrying.

"Are you hurt?" she shouted.

"A little bit. Not bad. Cold."

"I bet."

"Let us get you out of there." Still crouching, she shuffled back. "How are we going to do that?"

"Thanks for coming," he called. "I thought you would call Calie."

"I did. She's on her way."

"Emergency services?"

"Don't know. We need to get you out of the vehicle."

David came around the pickup's roof. The Subaru's head-lights cast him in silhouette.

"He's in there?" David said.

"Yes. Not hurt bad, but it looks like he can't move. Seat-belt is stuck."

David moved around.

"Should we smash the windshield?"

"They're pretty tough. It would take a whole lot of force and we'd end up hurting him."

"Right. Yeah." David looked along the roof. "Maybe we can rock it onto its wheels?"

"Again, too dangerous."

"So what would the paramedics do? Cut a hole in the roof?"

"They'd have the equipment. Remove the windshield maybe? Or..." Alicia trailed off, looking at the passenger side of the pickup. Effectively the roof.

With two doors in it.

"Give me a leg up," she said.

"What now?"

"Don't worry."

She scrambled up herself. Somehow. Not even thinking about it. The pickup rocked.

"Sheesh, Alicia," David said. "You're going to hurt yourself."

"Maybe." It wasn't easy balancing. She stayed on hands and knees. Standing on the back door, she took the latch of the front door. Lifted it.

"What are you trying to do?" David said.

"Open this up. Then I can get down to him."

"What? Like a trapdoor."

"Yes." She got the door up a little. It was heavy, and her angle was bad.

She needed something to wedge into it. She whipped off one of her shoes and jammed it in.

"Get me a rock or something," she said. "A board or a some piece of wood. Something to help hold the door open."

"I don't understand."

"Something solid. Just get it. There must be something."

"Will do."

From the corner of her eye, Alicia saw David's phone flashlight come on.

She lifted the door a little more. The angle was all wrong. The weight was way more than she'd been expecting.

"You should get down," Brent said from inside the pickup. "No sense in you getting hurt too."

"I won't get hurt."

"At the very least you're going to pull a muscle lifting that door."

"I'll be fine. You sit tight."

"Thanks for coming," he said. "My phone. It was..."

"You don't need to explain. We'll have you soon."

She wished she was as confident as she hoped she sounded. The door was heavy. She really had no idea how she was going to actually safely get to him.

But she had to try.

Chapter Forty

Alicia watched David's phone flashlight shone around the road near the fallen pickup as he looked for a rock suitable for wedge the door open.

"We should talk this through," Brent said, below Alicia, lying against the driver's door. "You need ropes and pulleys. Use them to pull open the door."

"We don't have ropes."

"There should be some in my toolbox in the pickup's tray."

"I bet. Locked?" Alicia's arms were tiring, holding the passenger door up.

"Of course."

"Where is the key?"

"With my fob."

"Which is in your hand?"

"Yes."

"I'll be down with you in a second. You can give it to me then. How can this door be so heavy? I open car doors all the time. Has your truck got lead bulletproofing or something?"

Brent actually laughed.

"Just the angle," he said. "Mostly you're opening car doors horizontally, not vertically."

"Yes, yes, I understand all that. I'm just complaining aloud about some guy who likes to get attention from a woman by rolling his truck out in the middle of some endless forest."

"That's me. Craving attention every moment."

David came back, shining his flashlight and holding up a rock the size of his fist.

"Good." She took it and wedged into the door, holding it open.

"More?" he said.

"Yes. A bigger one. I'll work my way along."

"All right then." David turned and went looking again.

But then Alicia realized that it was all very well to wedge the door, but as soon as she lifted it again, the rock would fall.

Right on Brent.

Not a good plan.

She cursed.

"You could use it to smash the back passenger window," Brent said. "I won't get much glass on me."

"No. I've got a better idea."

Alicia took the rock out, but held the door open..

She crouched, getting her feet right in onto the door pillar. She got a good grip on the door.

Taking a couple of breaths, she pushed up. Lifting the door as high as she could.

Then she saw what she'd done.

She was upright. Holding the door in place. But she couldn't move it any farther.

The door had gone as far as it would. Up to its normal opening stopper plates or whatever they were called. The hinge shape that stopped the door from going all the way forward onto the pickup's fender.

She cursed.

"Language," David said. "Dad's turning in his grave."

"I know it. Shut up and get up here and help me."

"What?"

"Stand up on the fender and we can break this stupid hinge and lay the door down."

"Huh?"

"Get up on the front wheel!"

"None of this is a very good idea," Brent said from inside the car.

"Shut up and let us rescue you."

"I don't need rescuing."

"Right. How long have you been lying there? Against the cold ground. In the dark. Trying to cut your seatbelt with–what is that?–a key?"

"Yeah. My knife is in the glove compartment. On the positive side, I did manage to get my insurance and registration, so when the cops come, I'm all set."

"You're hilarious, you know that. Laugh a minute."

The pickup rocked some more as David climbed up across the chassis.

"I'm tending toward agreeing with him," David said. "Bad idea. It'll end in tears. Let's wait for the experts to get here."

"You can wait. But while you're waiting, just help me with this door a moment. Can you do that?"

"Yeah, yeah."

Somehow David reached around and got his hands on the bottom of the door.

"Now push," he said. "Don't drop it, I'm going to lose a finger."

Alicia pushed. She walked her hands down the window glass and the door's interior paneling. She had to step onto the side of the passenger seat. And stretch her other foot out to the edge of the dash by the air vent.

The door's hinge made a terrible sound.

The door jerked forward.

Beyond it, David scrabbled around.

"All right?" Alicia said.

"Just. Almost slipped off." David was kneeling on the fender, one foot back on the pickup's front tire.

"This is why you call emergency services," Brent said.

"Pipe down, you," Alicia said. "David, you okay?"

"Yeah, yeah. I'm climbing down."

"I'm going to get Brent."

"Good. Watch out you don't fall on him."

Alicia looked down. She should have opened the pickup's back door. Then she could have climbed down into the crew seating and reached around for Brent.

But it had been hard enough getting this door open. She wasn't about to try for the rear door now.

So she clambered down. One foot against the rise of the driveshaft or gearbox housing. One foot on the steering column.

She reached and tried Brent's seatbelt release. It didn't budge.

"There's a knife in the glove compartment?" she said.

"Should be."

Even with the glow from the Subaru's headlights shining through the pickup's cab, the glove compartment was in shadow. Alicia felt around. She found a kind of multitool thing in a leather satchel. She popped the dome and took a look at the tool.

With her thumb, she started to open the blade. Stopped.

She was balanced over Brent. Not an ideal footing to be holding a sharp knife.

Carefully she climbed right on down. Stood on the ground by his head.

Steady, she opened the blade and found the spot where he'd been working on the seatbelt with the key.

"You made some headway," she said. "But I think it would have taken you a week."

"I was willing to make that commitment."

"Of course." Alicia actually laughed.

The blade on the multitool was sharp, but Alicia still had to work hard to cut through the seatbelt strap. It was kind of reassuring, that the things were so strong.

Soon she had it separated, and Brent slumped away from

its support. Alicia slipped the end through the lock clasp slider and got him free. Got him around and up to his feet.

There wasn't a whole lot of space for them.

They stood, pressed up together.

"Are you hurt?" she said, almost breathless.

"Little bit," he said. "Leg. Head."

"Lips?" she said.

"What?"

She snorted at herself. "Just being corny. I'm glad you're all right."

She peered into his eyes. In the soft, filtered light from the Subaru's headlights he looked even more gorgeous than she remembered.

"We should get out of here," she said, even if just to stop herself from drifting off into a dream.

"We should," he said.

"You go first," she said. "I'll help you up."

"No, you go."

"This is not an argument. I know it's your job, but right now, you're the person getting rescued."

He smiled. She just wanted to kiss those lips.

"All right," he said, and bent just a little closer.

Then she had her arms around him. Her lips on his. Eager and insistent.

And he was giving it right back.

Then she was off and caught up in it. His body against hers. Tingles and tugs through every nerve. His hands on her back. On her hips.

Her hands exploring too.

"Hey!" David shouted from outside. "What's going on in there. Come on. This is a car wreck. There's no time for that kind of shenanigans."

Alicia and Brent broke contact and Alicia looked around.

There was David, standing just beyond the windshield, shining his phone flashlight at them.

"I'll go first then," Brent said, stroking her cheek with the back of his fingers clearly charged with static and pheromones.

"We can discuss this later," she said.

"At length." He grinned.

Outside, David shouted, "For the love everything, just get out!"

David and Alicia laughed, and she guided him as he climbed up on the seats and gear lever and clambered on out of the pickup.

Chapter Forty-One

It was two days later when Brent arrived at Alicia and David's father's house on Bondurant Street in Candleton.

The skies were clear and the air had an actual warmth to it. Perhaps Alicia was acclimatizing. Wouldn't that be something?

Getting used to Alaska.

It wasn't so bad really.

Brent had called ahead, so she knew he was on his way. She hadn't seen him since Calie had arrived at the site of the wreck and administered to him like a mother taking care of a toddler with a stubbed toe.

But they'd talked. Texted. Emailed.

Strengthening that connection. He hadn't been too badly hurt, and his recovery had been fast.

"Hey," he said now, at the door to her father's house. He

was dressed in a dark blue button shirt, jeans and heavy tan work boots. She could have just stripped him right there. Right on the veranda.

But she got herself in check and stepped back to usher him into the house.

"Thanks again," he said, stepping across the threshold. "For rescuing me. I haven't said it properly in person."

"Well," she said, "I guess that makes us even."

"Even? Oh. The blazing wreck of your airliner from which I heroically plucked you to safety."

She laughed and put her hand on his chest.

"That's it," she said. His body was firm.

"It's hardly the same," he said, guiding his own hand to her elbow. Slipping it around her back.

She tingled.

He was so close. He smelled musky. Manly.

She gazed into his eyes, sure that she would vanish into them any moment.

"See," he said, "I would have gotten out of the pickup just fine. Walked out to the highway and hitchhiked home. You on the other hand would have been turned to charcoal."

She snorted. "My friend, you are exaggerating *both* instances. Suit yourself. I suppose that this is what you tell your fishing buddies."

His smile faded a little. "No. The only exaggerations there are about the size of the fish."

"Especially the ones that get away."

"I don't let them get away," he said.

Then her lips were on his and that fire ran through her

again. They pressed in so close. Hips to hips, chest to chest. Arms wrapped.

A little thought trickled through her head, that David was out at the courthouse finalizing things, and he might be away for another hour.

Brent pulled back a little and stared at her. He had a day's stubble, which, if she was honest, looked great on him.

He kept his hands on her hips and she kept her hands on his upper arms.

"Feel like we should dance," she said. "While we have the chance. I could put on some music."

"That would be nice. But first I want to ask you about something."

"Oh?"

"So I know you'll be going back to Oklahoma sometime. Sooner than later, right? Work calls. Your father's estate will be resolved. Nothing holding you here."

"Well, something."

"Me?"

"Yes."

He smiled, but it was kind of sad. "And I couldn't ask you to stay. Not at all."

"It's up to me."

"I have another idea, though. Which you might, I don't know, find a bit... forward."

"Forward?" She flicked her eyes at the stairway. Gave a little nod. A little wink. There were bedrooms upstairs.

He grinned. "Not like that."

"I was teasing. Which is unfair of me. We know this has

been nice, and I hope that we can stay in touch, but I think bed would be a bad idea."

He nodded, actually agreeing. "It would leave us with the wrong kind of end here. But it doesn't have to end here."

"Brent."

"Okay, I just want to run an idea by you."

"Should I sit down?"

They were still standing in the house's little foyer.

Why was her heart fluttering? There was nothing he could suggest that would be practical.

"It won't take but a moment. I was thinking that I could come to Oklahoma. I mean, my skills and training are real transportable. And Tulsa International Airport actually has some openings and..."

Alicia had stopped listening to the details. There was a buzzing in her head. An odd, warm, uplifting buzz. Like some kind of drug.

Like her brain flooding with endorphins and dopamine and whatever other feel-good chemicals there were.

"Alicia?" he said.

"Sorry?" She focused on his face.

"I was saying, that there were options. And, well, I've found a place I can stay."

"A place you can stay?"

"A little condo. It's in Park Downs, which is—"

"Oh, no. You don't want to stay there."

"Really? The lease looks pretty good."

"I bet it does. No, I'll find you a place. Close to me and..." she trailed off.

There was no question. How funny. She hadn't even had to think about it.

He would move out to Oklahoma.

"What did I miss?" he said, the slightest of smiles on his lips.

"Are you for real?"

"Pinch me and see."

"No. You pinch me, because I must be dreaming."

"How about this instead?" he said, and leaned forward to kiss her again.

Alicia slipped into it. He tasted so good. Felt so good against her. Strong and firm, but supple too.

She shuddered.

Pushed away.

"That," she said, "is no way to make a woman feel as if she's not dreaming."

Brent laughed.

"What about a car, though? Are you going to drive?"

He laughed again. "You're serious. You think me coming to Oklahoma is a good idea?"

"Mister, remember a moment ago?"

"Kissing?"

"Exactly. Did I seem to offer any suggestion that it was a bad idea?"

"You might have been living for the moment."

"Always, but also with an eye to the future."

"You think we might have a future?"

She nodded slowly.

"We do. We definitely do. And I just realized that you

totaled your pickup."

"Not totaled, but it was bad. Calie's taking it off my hands to fix up. So I will need to get a new..." Brent turned toward the open front door.

David stood there. Right on the veranda step.

"Don't mind me," he said. "Just eavesdropping."

"How long have you been there!" Alicia yelled.

"Long enough. It's so sweet! But I actually managed to avoid gagging." He held up a sheaf of papers. "And the house here is cleared. They're not taking it away. The condos will be smaller, and perhaps less offensive."

"Really!"

"Well, there are still some hoops to jump through, but it looks as if the city has either backed down or made an error or had a change of heart. Hardly matters what. The point is that there's no hurry now. I can stay up here and potter along with it. As long as I like." David came up across the veranda and closed the door behind him. "So let's keep the heat in, huh?" He gave Alicia a wink.

"So funny. But what, you're staying?"

"For a while, at least. Someone's got to take care of Drumlin. I've talked to Francine and the kids and they might come up for an extended vacation."

"Alaska's a big commitment," Brent said. "Don't let this mild fall weather fool you. There'll be ten feet of snow out there in three months."

"So we're talking about big commitments, huh?" David said, stepping in close to Brent. "You break her heart and I'm going to come and tear yours out."

"Hey!" Alicia said. "I don't need my brother muscling in like that. I'm perfectly capable of tearing out his heart by myself. But, *awww, so sweet.*"

"Huh," Brent said. "You two take some getting used to."

"Yeah we do," David said. He tapped Brent's sternum with his index finger, but added a wink. "I'm going to find a bottle of wine, or a beer to celebrate. I mean celebrate the house, not whatever this is." He waved the same index finger between Alicia and Brent.

"We can celebrate both," Alicia said.

"Yeah, yeah." David said, walking along the hallway toward the kitchen.

Alicia looked back at Brent. He stared back at her.

She took his hands.

"Are you sure?" she said. "I don't want half-measures."

"No half-measures. All in."

"All in."

"I'll give notice at work. I'll sell my place. Fly out with you."

A tingle ran through Alicia. From her scalp to her toes.

"You're for real."

"You bet."

She grinned and grabbed him. Dragged him closer.

"Then we'd better get started huh?"

"You bet."

She kissed him then. Long and strong and deep, and she knew it was going to work out.

Afterword

Thanks for reading *Wilkes Landing*. I hope you enjoyed the book as much as I enjoyed writing it.

You'll see from my 'also by' pages here that for the most part I'm a writer of science fiction and thrillers and even fantasy. It's true, this is my first out and out romance novel, though I would like to think that there are many romantic elements to most of those other works.

I also like to think that I read across the spectrum. In that mix there are plenty of romance novels. In general, they're well-written with engaging stories and characters whose lives are in flux and conflict. They're struggling with their desires and emotions.

I hope that I've hit those marks with my story here. That I've gotten the story beats right for the passionate readers of romances.

And as I writer I know I'm always striving to do better

with my next book. So, while this is my first foray into a straightforward romance, I can already feel the brooding niggles in my writing sessions of wanting to create more stories.

There are even a couple of characters right here in *Wilkes Landing* that I kind of figure deserve a little more romance in their lives. Calie for one. Maybe even Red. I enjoyed the setting and the folks making their homes in Wilkes Landing, and Candleton. I think that maybe I'd like to spend some more time in those places and see if the sparks fly.

Thanks again for reading. Feel free to stop by the website and say hi. It's always good to hear from readers.

Sean

October 2025

Acknowledgments

I am ever grateful to Vera Soroka for her helpful insights into an earlier version of this novel. Check out Vera's romances too. A whole lot saucier than mine here, but she has some great series.

As always, any mistakes in the book remain mine.

About the Author

A frequent traveler from his home in New Zealand, Sean Monaghan has made it to thirty-one countries so far, all providing rich settings for his stories, which run the spectrum from thrillers to science fiction to literary, and even romance. Having made numerous visits to the U.S. Sean likes to think he knows his way around.

His stories have won the Jim Baen Memorial Award, the Amazing Stories Award, the Sir Julius Vogel Award and the Asimov's Readers' Poll Award, among others.

Sean writes from a nook in the corner of his 110 year old character home.

www.seanmonaghan.com

instagram.com/seanmonaghanauthor
facebook.com/seanmonaghanauthor

Also by Sean Monaghan

CAPTAIN ARLON STODDARD ADVENTURES

Asteroid Jumpers

Ice Hunters

Ship Tracers

Core Runners

Desert Creepers

Underworld Climbers

Island hoppers

Mist Drifters

Dead Ringers

Tramp Steamers

Cradle Robbers

Margin Dwellers

CAPTAIN ARLON STODDARD Shorts

Ortanide Steppers (novella)

Sea Skimmers (short story)

Dark Behemoth (short story)

KARNISH RIVER NAVIGATIONS

Arlchip Burnout

Canal Days

Eastern Foray

Guest House Izarra

Jackpot Kingdom

Liquid Machine

Night Operations

Persephone Quest

Rorqual Saitu

Tombs Under Vaile

Waxing Xebec

Yesterday's Ziggurat

THE JUPITER FILES

Book 1: Deuterium Shine

Book 2: Tritium Blaze

STANDALONE SCIENCE FICTION

The Ergs

Raphael Marooned

Hanging Vines

Raven Rising

Athena Setting

The City Builders

The Cly

Gretel

SCIENCE FICTION SHORT STORY COLLECTIONS

Balance

Balance II

Balance III

*Un*Balanced

Listen, You!

OTHER COLLECTIONS

Arms Wide

One Degree Below Freezing

Landslide Country

STANDALONE THRILLERS

The Courier

Ice Fracture

Rotations

Taken by Surprise

EMILY JADE SERIES

Big Sur

Glass Bay

COLE WRIGHT THRILLERS

The Arrival

Measured Aggression

Hide Away

Slow Burn

Scorpion Bait

Sail Man

CONTEMPORARY SHORT STORIES

Single Branch, With Blossom

The Umbrellas of Tokyo

Concentration

CONTEMPORARY NOVELS

This is the Perfect Way To Wake

Steel Wagons

MORGENFELD

The Mapmaker of Morgenfeld

The Stairs at Cronnenwood

The Chimneys in Atterton

The Wintermas Paintings

The Bergeron Sculptures

The Ingersal Ballet